The Pastor's Wife

THE PASTOR'S WIFE

Jennifer AlLee

Abingdon Press fiction
a novel approach to faith

Nashville, Tennessee

The Pastor's Wife

Copyright © 2010 by Jennifer AlLee

ISBN-13: 978-1-4267-0225-9

Published by Abingdon Press, P.O. Box 801, Nashville, TN 37202

www.abingdonpress.com

All rights reserved.

The persons and events portrayed in this work of fiction are the
creations of the author, and any resemblance to persons living or
dead is purely coincidental.

Cover design by Anderson Design Group, Nashville, TN

Library of Congress Cataloging-in-Publication Data

AlLee, Jennifer.
  The pastor's wife / Jennifer AlLee.
     p. cm.
  ISBN 978-1-4267-0225-9 (pbk. : alk. paper)
  I. Title.
  PS3601.I39P37 2010
  813'.6—dc22

2009046249

Printed in the United States of America

1 2 3 4 5 6 7 8 9 10 / 15 14 13 12 11 10

To all the pastors' wives who minister every day in their own unique ways, but especially to my friends Karen, Robin, and Amy. You inspire me with your genuine love for God and His people.

Acknowledgments

Writing often feels like a solitary task, but in truth, it's an amazing group effort. I humbly give thanks to the essential members of my group:

Editor extraordinaire, Barbara Scott. You encouraged me to stretch and grow, to push past where I thought I could go. Thanks a thousand times for your support and for seeing the potential in my little story.

Patti Lacy, who rescued me when I was a sobbing mess and mentored me for a year. I learned so much from you, not only about writing, but about reflecting the love of God.

Lisa Richardson. You started out as my critique partner, became my friend, and now you're the sister of my heart. I'm so glad God is letting us experience this crazy ride together!

American Christian Fiction Writers. I literally would not be here today without this incredible organization. What a blessing you've been in my life.

My husband, Marcus, and my son, Billy. What can I say? I love you both so very much. None of this would mean anything without you to share it with.

And finally, but most important, praise be to God, the creator of creativity and imagination. Thank you for the gift of storytelling and all the blessings you've showered on me.

1

"Hold the elevator!"

Maura Sullivan ran across the lobby as fast as she could in high-heeled pumps. Once again she second-guessed her choice of attire for this meeting. She didn't plan to stay in town long. Just get in, talk to the lawyer, and run out again. But in a place the size of Granger, Ohio, there was a good chance she'd run into someone she knew. And if that happened, she wanted them to see a successful, self-sufficient businessperson, not a frazzled woman barely holding it together.

The elevator doors were almost shut when they stopped, then slowly started to move in reverse. Maura sighed in relief. Maybe her luck had changed.

"Sorry," a male voice said from inside the car. "I couldn't find the right button and—"

The man in the elevator gaped at Maura, his finger glued to the button panel. Meanwhile, Maura's stomach fell to the tips of her shoes. If not for her impractical footwear, she'd be jogging up the stairs right now instead of staring like an idiot at her almost ex-husband.

So much for her luck. It was just as bad as ever.

"Maura?" He found his voice, but his body didn't move an inch.

"Hi, Nick." There were probably lots of things she should say, but none came to mind. Instead, she forced herself to take three steps forward and enter the elevator.

Nick's eyes never left her. His head just swiveled as she moved in next to him. He finally removed his finger from the "door open" button, letting his hand fall against his thigh with a slap. "What are you doing here?"

Trying not to faint. Telling myself I won't be sick. Both true, but neither facts she wished to share. "I have a meeting." She leaned around him and hit the second-floor button. The doors slid closed.

Nick squeezed the bridge of his nose with two fingers. "Is your meeting with Wendell Crowley?"

"Yes." Dread worked its way down her spine. How could he know that? She was clearly the last person he expected to see today. If he hadn't known she was coming to town, how could he know anything about her meeting?

Nick made an unintelligible noise and muttered to himself. "Great. How could she?"

"Look, I'm sorry we ran into each other like this." Maura's heart thudded in her chest as she tried to ease the tension in the small moving box. "I promise, as soon as I meet with the lawyer, I'll be out of here and you'll never see me again."

Nick looked at her, his eyes drawn together. "Afraid not."

"What?"

"Your escape won't be that neat and tidy." The elevator stopped, bounced, and the doors eased open. "We're going to the same meeting."

This had to be a joke.

Nick and Maura sat in matching chairs on one side of a heavy oak desk. On the other side sat Wendell Crowley, reading from the Last Will and Testament of Miss Harriet Lenore Granger. The elderly attorney had been a close personal friend of Miss Hattie's, making the reading of this particular will more emotional for him than most.

Nick was emotional, too, but for a completely different reason. As the lawyer read on, making less and less sense, Nick's fingers squeezed around the arms of his chair. Beside him, Maura's hands were clenched together in her lap so tightly that he could see her fingernails digging into her flesh. She was obviously just as shocked as he was.

Nick had spent a great deal of time with Miss Hattie in her last days, but she'd never alluded to what she planned in her will. Then again, maybe she had, in her own subtle way. He was at her bedside the night before she died, and as always, the woman encouraged him to hold on to hope.

"It's not too late for you," she'd said. "I know you're too stubborn to go after that wife of yours, but you never know . . . she just might come back to you."

Rather than argue he'd squeezed her hand and prayed with her. That night, his dear friend had died peacefully in her sleep.

Now that whole encounter took on new meaning in light of what Wendell had read. Maybe the woman's intentions were good, but it didn't make him happy about the outcome.

Nick glanced at Maura. She had a lot of nerve showing up in town after the way she left him. From the way she was dressed, she must be managing just fine in California. She didn't look so good now, though. The red blush that had stained her cheeks in the elevator was gone, replaced by skin so pale he thought she might faint. She wasn't dealing with the terms of the will any better than he was.

He turned to Wendell. "Let me see if I understand you correctly. Miss Hattie left Maura the Music Box Theatre, but there are two conditions."

Wendell smiled. "Yes."

"Would you repeat those conditions, please?"

"Certainly. First, the theatre must be used for at least one church function, such as a play or concert. Second, Maura must move into the church parsonage."

The room was quiet as a mime convention as Nick rolled that fact around in his head. "With me?" he finally asked.

Wendell didn't hesitate. "Yes. With you."

That snapped Maura out of her stupor. "Is this even legal?" Her voice was shrill, and she leaned so far forward, Nick feared she might fall out of her chair. "I mean, it's the kind of stunt they pull in soap operas. Can you really tell two people they have to live together as a condition of a will?"

"You can," Wendell answered. "And Miss Hattie did."

"But I can't," she sputtered. "I'm not . . . we're not . . . I just can't!"

The smile never left the man's face. "It's not a problem. After all, you two are still married."

"But we've been separated for six years." Maura's voice was almost a whisper, as if she were sharing a secret with the lawyer that the whole town wasn't already privy to.

"Yes, I know. But legally and in the eyes of God, you're still married." Wendell turned to Nick, lowering his head and looking over the edge of his tiny reading glasses.

Nick's eyes narrowed in response. It didn't take a genius to figure out that Miss Hattie hoped to reunite him and Maura. And it stood to reason she'd gone over her scheme with Wendell ahead of time to make sure everything was legal and in order. But charging two people to live and work together with no parameters didn't make sense. There must be something Wendell hadn't told them.

"I'm confused," Maura said. "Are you telling me that in order to own the theatre, I have to live in the parsonage for the rest of my life?"

Good question. Nick looked at the lawyer who shook his head.

"No, not at all." Wendell pointed to the will. "You only have to fulfill the conditions for six months. At that time, the property becomes yours free and clear."

"No strings attached?" Maura asked.

"None. At the end of six months, you can live wherever you want. You can even sell the building, if you're so inclined. Of course," he said with a dip of his head, "I hope you won't be."

Nick listened as Maura and Wendell talked about the property. She was actually considering going through with this crazy proposition. Nick's entire life was about to turn upside down, and it seemed he was powerless to stop it.

"Excuse me," he blurted, interrupting Wendell in mid-sentence. "What about me? Don't I have any say in this?"

The two looked as if they just remembered he was in the room. "Of course, you do," Wendell answered. "What in particular do you want to address?"

Nick looked pointedly at Maura. "What if I don't want her to live with me?"

She flinched, and Nick pushed away the guilt that tried to settle in his heart. He didn't want to hurt her, but he had to tell the truth. Besides, whatever discomfort she felt now couldn't compare to the pain he felt the night he came home to an empty house and a good-bye note on his pillow.

Wendell's eyebrows rose in surprise. "Naturally, you have the right to refuse to let Mrs. Shepherd—"

"Ms. Sullivan," she corrected him.

He nodded. "You can refuse to let her move into the parsonage. But if you do, it will nullify the will."

"Then what happens to the theatre?" Maura asked.

Wendell flipped over a few pages. "It would be sold, but I'm not at liberty to say what would be done with the proceeds." He turned to Nick. "By the way, did I mention that if the conditions are met, after six months the church will receive a sizable donation?"

Ah, here was the other shoe. Nick ground his teeth. "No, you did not mention that. Just how sizable?"

"Ten thousand dollars."

Nick crossed his arms and sat back hard against the seat. Ten thousand dollars might not seem like a lot to some folks, but to him, it was an answer to prayer—an answer Miss Hattie decided to help along. She knew all about the programs he wanted to implement, the staff he wanted to bring on, if only the money were there. She knew exactly how to get to him. He could endure six months of almost anything if it meant bringing much-needed funds into the church. Still, he didn't want to rush the decision.

"I need some time to think this over." Nick rose, ending the meeting.

Wendell stood with him. "I understand. In fact, I'd advise the two of you to go some place private so you can discuss the matter." The lawyer reached into his jacket pocket and pulled out a key ring, which he handed to Maura.

She took the keys as she stood up. "Are these for the theatre?"

"Yes. I think you should take a look at the place before you make your final decision." Wendell smiled as he walked them out of the office. "I know you have a lot to talk about. Please call me as soon as you come to an agreement."

Following behind Maura, Nick mulled over what had just happened. He had a feeling the meeting had gone exactly as the lawyer and Miss Hattie planned. Not only were Nick and Maura considering this weird arrangement, but they were leaving together to the theatre. After six years of living alone, it seemed his destiny was once again entangled with that of his wayward wife. And there wasn't a thing he could do to stop it.

2

Just look at this place. It's incredible!"

Maura stood in the middle of the old Music Box Theatre, with her arms flung wide, eyes sparkling. Nick watched as she walked farther down the aisle, reverently touching the backs of the old, dusty seats as though they were made of pure gold.

This was the first time Nick had been inside the old theatre. When he came to Granger as an idealistic twenty-four year old, excited about his new life as a pastor with his wife by his side, the Music Box was one of many boarded-up buildings on Main Street. Now at a mature thirty, here he stood, watching his estranged wife lust after the last property in town that still needed renovation.

Maura didn't seem the least bit daunted by the idea of inheriting a fixer-upper. "From the outside, you can't tell how large this space is. Look at the stage. It's big enough for full-blown productions."

Nick listened as she exclaimed over the orchestra pit, the ornate carvings that framed the stage, the murals on the walls and ceiling. Her hands flew as she gestured and raced from one part of the theatre to the next.

The guarded, defensive woman who walked back into his life a few hours before had vanished. Now she was animated, full of enthusiasm, and excited about the possibilities that stood in front of her.

Nick's gut twisted at her transformation into the woman he had married. Living in the same house with her would be hard enough if she continued playing the role of ice princess. But if she warmed up and started acting like the woman he fell in love with, the next six months would be sheer torture. He had to find a way to talk her out of this.

"You know," he called, walking up the aisle to meet her, "it's going to take a lot of work to get this place back into shape. Not to mention it might not be up to code. You could be looking at some serious structural issues."

Maura shook her head, still taking in her surroundings. "No, it's fine."

"How can you be so sure?"

She squatted down in the middle of a row, disappearing from view. Nick wondered how she managed the move in that suit she wore.

"Weren't you paying attention at Wendell's office?" Her disembodied voice traveled to him through the musty air. "Miss Hattie had it checked out before she completed her will. The place is structurally sound. The major issues are cosmetic." She popped up into view, swiping the back of her hand across her forehead. "It'll just take a little work to make the place shine again."

"A little work? Did you notice the paint peeling off the walls? And there's at least an inch of dust on these seats." He hit one hard with his palm, just to prove his point. Although the small puff of dust that rose into the air was not what he had hoped for, he was strangely pleased when the entire back of the seat fell off with a clatter, hitting the armrest of the seat behind it and knocking it off as well.

"You just broke two of my seats!" Maura jammed her fists onto her hips and scowled at him.

Nick took a step back. "Actually, I may have just saved a life. What if someone sat there and the seat fell apart? You should be thanking me. You could have gotten sued on opening night."

She shook her head and groaned. "Nobody would have sat in that seat, Nick, because I intend to have them all checked out and repaired well before opening night. Do you really think I'm that irresponsible?"

"No, of course not." This wasn't turning out the way he'd hoped. He didn't want to insult her, only discourage her a bit and convince her to give up this insane plan. "My point is there's more than a little work to be done before the place will be fit to open to the public. I just want to make sure you're looking at the big picture."

Maura laughed. "Well, this is different. Since when do you look at the bleak side of life? What happened to mister the-sun-is-always-shining-somewhere-in-the-world?"

"Having my wife walk out on me must have dampened my optimism."

That sobered her. She hugged her arms around her chest and looked him in the eye. "You left me long before I left you."

Her accusation pierced his heart like a poison-tipped dart. All he'd ever done was his job, a job she knew he loved when she married him. And she'd left him for doing his job well. It would be so much easier to move on and ignore their past—pretend none of it had happened. But he couldn't let it go. "Don't you think it's time we talked about it?"

"No." The word shot out of her like a bullet, and her gaze dropped to the floor. When she looked back at him, determination blazed in her eyes.

"You and I have gone through a lot in the last few years," she said quietly. "I know it might be impossible for you to believe, but I never wanted to hurt you and I still don't. I have no idea why Miss Hattie thought she could manipulate us back together, but she did, and we're stuck with it. The plain truth is that I want to make this theatre work. I *need* to make it work."

He should leave it at that. She'd made it clear she didn't want to talk about their past. To get further involved in her current life, the life she chose to live alone, would only lead to trouble. But Nick had never been a passive bystander.

"Why would you care about running some little theatre in a hick town? I thought you liked living in California. If you want to run a business so badly, why don't you wait until your father hands over the coffee shop?"

She blanched, and he wished he could recall his words. He had no idea what she'd been doing over the last six years, but he knew before she spoke that it hadn't been easy.

"My father died two months ago." Her words were flat, as though she'd already expended so much energy on the subject she refused to use any more. "He did leave me the coffee shop, and a mountain of debt along with it."

"Maura, I'm sorry, I—"

She held up her hand. "It's okay. I won't bore you with the details. Let's just say the one bright spot it the situation was that Da bought a prime piece of land well before it was prime, and it's completely paid for. In fact, I've had several generous offers on it already."

"So you're planning to sell?"

"I thought about it, but I wasn't sure. Not until today. See, while I can make a profit on the land, after I pay all the bills, there won't be enough to start another business, or even buy another house in California." He must have looked confused because she continued. "Da and I lived in the apartment over the shop, remember?"

"Sure, of course, I do." From the first day Nick had walked into Sullivan's Coffee Shop and watched Maura take care of a rude customer, he'd known she was the one. He'd eaten countless bowls of their signature chowder as an excuse to come by and get to know her.

When Nick picked her up for their first date, Joe Sullivan grilled him as though they'd never met, despite their many casual conversations over a cup of coffee or a bowl of chowder. The genial coffee shop proprietor became a bit more imposing when Nick changed from a customer into the man who was dating Joe's only daughter.

Thinking back on that time, something clicked in Nick's head. Something he hadn't thought about in years. "This was your dream."

Maura's eyes narrowed. "What?"

"To own a theatre. Remember our first date?"

Her face softened, and she nodded. "I remember."

"We talked about our goals, and one of yours was to own a theatre someday." Other memories from that day came back in a rush: licking ice-cream cones as they walked on the beach, the warmth of her hand in his, how beautiful she looked with her thick black hair whipping in the wind. Nick pushed the images aside, refusing to let nostalgia carry him away. "Is that why you're so gung ho to do this?"

"Hardly. I gave up silly dreams like that a long time ago." She rubbed the back of her neck, grimacing. "The truth is Sullivan's hasn't been a profitable business for a long time. A family-owned shop can't compete with the national chains. For the past few months, I've been debating what to do, trying to figure out how to pay all the bills and still keep Sullivan's open. Then Wendell called and told me about the will. Of course, he wouldn't tell me what I would inherit—only that it was significant. I hoped whatever Miss Hattie left me would help me start over somewhere else." Maura laughed, but there was no joy in the sound. "I had no idea I'd be starting over *here*. Guess the joke's on me."

Despite their history, despite the hurt he still felt, Nick's heart went out to her. He wanted to encourage her, to tell her that everything would be all right. But that was a promise he couldn't make.

"So you're sure about this?" he asked. "You're absolutely certain you want to take over this theatre?"

"You bet I am. Once I sell the coffee shop and pay the bills, I should have enough money left over to get this place back in shape. I'm not sure what I'll do after that, but at least now I have some hope for the future."

Hope for the future. Boy, God sure did work in some wild, ironic ways. "I guess this is an answer to prayer for you."

"*You* would probably call it that."

Nick trod lightly. "What would you call it?"

"Luck. Coincidence. I have no idea. What I do know is that if I want to get anywhere in this life, I've got to take care of myself." She let her arms fall to her side and walked back up the aisle toward the door. "I've seen enough," she said without looking back. "Let's go to Wendell's and finalize this."

So that was it. She'd made up her mind. Nick knew her well enough to realize that no amount of discussion would sway her. He should be furious at her for making a decision that would affect them both without asking what he thought. He should be concerned about how his life would change now that they'd be sharing a house. He should refuse to make his heart available for more pain and rejection. But none of that seemed as important as the bigger issue at hand. For a moment, he'd caught a glimpse of the hurt that went straight to her core and wounded her soul. Maura was in the midst of a crisis of faith, and right now, all Nick could focus on was helping her patch things up with God.

Maura took a deep breath. Slowly and carefully, she signed her name on the bold line at the bottom of the contract. With that simple act, she took temporary control of the Music Box Theatre until such time, after all stipulations were met, that ownership would be permanently transferred to her. Just some ink on a page, and her life was now turned totally around.

"Fine. That's just fine." Wendell smiled broadly. "I'll check in on the two of you from time to time, just to see how you're progressing, but I don't foresee any problems." He turned to Maura. "I expect you'll need to put your affairs in order in California before you can get settled here. Is there anything I can help you with?"

Maura shook her head. "Nothing comes to mind. As I told Nick, I'm sure I can sell the shop quickly, and there's no need for me to be there while escrow closes. I should be back in Granger in a few weeks."

"Wonderful." Wendell shook her hand, then turned and shook Nick's. "It was good seeing you again, Pastor Shepherd. Feel free to call me if you need anything."

Maura and Nick left the office and headed down the stairs. With each step, another doubt assailed her. Had she done the right thing? Had she been too rash, too headstrong? She had just made a huge decision after giving it little consideration.

She thought it was her only option, but was that true? Running the theatre meant moving back to Granger, a place she barely wanted to visit let alone live. What had she gone and done?

By the time they got to the parking lot, Maura was in a full-on panic attack. Nick was saying something, but with all the buzzing in her head he sounded like he was talking through a fast-food drive-up speaker. She walked to her rental car, put her hands on the hood, and hyperventilated.

The buzzing grew louder, droning in her ears like a cloud of mosquitoes circling her head. Finally, she made out one word, repeated over and over. "Breathe." She felt a hand on the back of her neck, gently rubbing away the tension—heard the soothing voice telling her to breathe, breathe, breathe. Eventually, her breath evened out and the mosquitoes flew away. She was now completely aware of Nick's strong hand kneading her neck and shoulders, and his reassuring voice that continued to encourage her. It struck her that not only had she broken out in a cold sweat, but tears were streaming down her face. So much for offering up the appearance of a confident businesswoman.

"I'm okay," she said, pushing herself off the car hood and straightening up. "Do you have a—" Before she could finish the sentence, Nick held out a pocket pack of tissues. After she'd wiped her face and blown her nose, she turned back to him. "Sorry. I'm not sure where that came from."

Nick shrugged. "It's been an emotional day. You probably needed a good cry."

She nodded. "I just hope I made the right decision. Now that it's official, it's kind of scary."

"Yes, it is. But things will get better."

"How? We've got to live together now. For six months. How are we going to do that?"

She waited for Nick to give her a definitive answer. To tell her exactly how everything would work out. But he didn't do that.

"I don't know," he said, looking as lost as she was. "We'll just have to take each day as it comes. We'll work it out."

Did he really believe that? And why was he being so nice to her? His life was about to be thrown into chaos too. It would be just like when they first moved to Granger, only different. They would be living together almost like a husband and wife, except they were nothing of the kind anymore. Through no desire of their own, they were about to return to the place where their world had fallen apart.

She looked into his eyes. They were stormy now, like the sky over the ocean. Once, she had believed every word he said. Once, she hadn't thought twice about trusting him. But that had blown up in her face.

How could she start trusting him now?

Maura shook herself. "Thank you for . . . thank you." She took a key on a plastic card out of her purse and unlocked the car door.

Nick cocked an eyebrow at her. "Where are you going?"

"To the Holiday Inn by the airport. My flight leaves first thing in the morning."

"I see." He turned from her, looking in the direction of the theatre. When he looked back, his jaw was set and his eyes had gone cold. "You never intended on staying past that meeting, did you?"

She shook her head slowly. "No, I sure didn't."

3

Selling her home and business was easier than Maura antici-
pated. But it was still hard.

Upon returning from Granger, she immediately called one
of the shop regulars, who was a commercial real estate agent.
As she expected, he knew of several prospective buyers for the
property. By the end of the week, Sullivan's had a "sold" sign in
the parking lot and a "closed" sign hanging on the front door.

Getting rid of the contents of Sullivan's had been more
traumatic. Maura hired a company to handle the estate sale.
But the morning of the sale, she couldn't tear herself away.
Something inside her needed to see who would end up with
the pieces of her life.

To see people paw through the contents of her home was
a little disconcerting. She had no use for the tall, green satin
leprechaun hat she'd found in the storage room, but it still
bothered her when a woman with a fanny pack picked it up
and said to no one in particular, "This is the tackiest thing I've
ever seen."

Maura wanted to snatch the hat right out of the woman's
hand. It was tacky, but Da had loved it.

"How much for the dart board?"

Turning around, Maura saw a young man talking to one of the company employees. He probably attended the college nearby, the same one Nick had gone to, and was looking for something to put up in his dorm room. A sad smile tugged at the corners of her mouth. Nick had tried to shoot darts a couple of times with some of the regulars at Sullivan's. It hadn't been pretty. A sad smile came to her lips. Except for that one time.

As the dart board buyer considered his purchase, another woman haggled over the price of a dozen old-fashioned straw holders. Behind her, someone pushed a button on the ancient jukebox Da had kept stocked with Irish favorites. The strains of Van Morrison singing "Tura Lura Lural" filled the air, and for a moment, Maura couldn't breathe.

She'd had enough. With a sigh, she made her way through the throng of bargain shoppers. It was time to let the past go.

The next morning, Maura took a final look at the place that had been her home for most of her life. As she stood in the parking lot, a geyser of sadness bubbled up inside, confusing her. Why was she so sad now? It was just a building, after all. She'd faced greater losses in her life: her mother's death from cancer when Maura was sixteen, and Da going to be with his beloved wife just a few months ago. Losing them was far more difficult than leaving a building.

Still, standing in front of the shop for the last time, Maura's emotions roiled. The new owners planned to demolish the building, replacing it with something new and trendy designed to bring in more revenue. Maura couldn't argue with the business sense of that plan, but it still made her heart ache. Sullivan's was small and simple, but it was home. Seeing it go was a little like losing her father all over again.

With the car packed to the brim with her personal items she hit the road, determined to adopt a positive outlook. The first time she'd made this drive, she was a bright-eyed newlywed. Though she expected to see the country they drove through, stopping to poke along the way, Nick had other ideas. They had to keep to the schedule, which meant side trips were nonexistent. But this time, it would be different. She had her route mapped out and a box on the passenger seat filled with CDs from her favorite movie musicals and Broadway shows. She was her own pilot, copilot, and navigator. There was no one to tell her how far to drive, where to stop, or what she could or couldn't see. And she planned to see all the interesting little tourist traps along the way.

The live unicorn exhibit was a huge disappointment and a total waste of time—just one more thing that didn't live up to her expectations.

"People really shouldn't be allowed to post blatantly false advertisements on the side of the road," she muttered to herself. Keeping her eyes forward with one hand on the steering wheel, she fiddled with the CD player. She punched a button and Julie Andrews's voice sang out, smooth as warm honey, claiming that all she wanted was a room somewhere.

Maura groaned. A room. It was getting late, and her little side trip had put her even further off schedule. She needed to find a hotel to stay the night, but right now all that greeted her was prairie as far as the eye could see. Her idea to remain spontaneous hadn't worked out well. The last two nights she'd had to try several hotels before she found one with a vacancy. Hopefully, tonight she'd get a room at the first hotel she found. Considering her luck lately, the owner would be a psychopath running another Bates Hotel. No wonder Nick had been such a stickler about planning ahead and keeping to the schedule when the two of them made this trip.

What was Nick doing now? Was he having dinner at home alone? More likely, she'd find him at some church function. But wherever he was, at least he had a bed to sleep in at the end of the day. Maura just hoped she'd find a place to stretch out and get some sleep. And soon.

—∞∞—

Maura made much better time after the unicorn incident, but her spirits hadn't improved any. By the time she arrived in Granger two days later, her joints felt locked in place and her muscles protested every move she made. Glancing at the seat beside her, Maura shuddered. It would be quite a while before she listened to any of those CDs again.

She drove down Main Street and made a right on Clover Ridge Road. Faith Community Church stood proud and tall, taking up the corner, sparkling in a relatively fresh new coat of white paint. Next to the church sat the parsonage, the first in a street full of modest, almost identical houses. Maura pulled into the driveway, cut the engine, and eased herself out of the car.

Standing out front, *deja vu* wound around her like a python, creeping up her body, slowly squeezing the air out of her. The first time she'd seen this house, Nick had been by her side. They were both excited and ready to embark on a new adventure. But while Maura looked at the parsonage, thinking of the home they would make together, Nick couldn't tear his eyes away from the church next door. That should have been her first clue.

When she left Granger, she swore she was done with the town and everyone in it. Now here she was, returning to the place where everything went so wrong. How ironic that in order to start a new life for herself, she had to backtrack into her old one.

She took a deep breath, climbed the three steps to the front porch, and reached out her hand. Her fingers stopped just short of the front door. She lived here, too, now. But just letting herself in didn't feel right, and ringing the bell felt way too formal. Finally, she gave the door a couple of awkward raps with her knuckles.

A moment later the door swung open and Nick stood in front of her, a frown creasing his forehead. "Maura. You're early."

She glanced at her watch. She'd called last night to update him on her progress. Naturally, she'd gotten the answering machine. But in her message, she'd only said that she'd arrive today. "I don't remember telling you what time I'd be in."

"You didn't."

"Then how can I be early?"

Nick shook his head. "I'm sorry. Of course, you're not. I just meant that I'm not ready for you yet."

Not ready in what way? She was afraid to ask. "Do you want me to come back later?"

"No. I mean, I'm just wrapping up a meeting. Come on in."

Nick stepped back, opening the door wider. Maura walked by him into the living room. A young woman in jeans and a T-shirt sprang off the couch, her blond ponytail bobbing.

Maura took a step backward. "I'm sorry if I'm interrupting anything—"

"No!" Nick and the blond spoke at once.

Nick cleared his throat. "No, really, everything's fine. Maura, this is Lainie Waters, our new youth director." He motioned with his hand between the two women. "Lainie, this is Maura. I told you about her."

Maura snapped her head in Nick's direction. What exactly did he tell this woman about her? More important, why did he feel the need to tell her anything?

Lainie bounded forward, doing a little dance around the coffee table, her hand extended. "So nice to meet you, Maura."

Not wanting to be impolite, Maura took her hand. "Likewise."

"Don't worry, I was just on my way out. We were having a meeting about the youth group, and by we I mean Pastor Nick, Pastor Chris, and I. Have you met Pastor Chris? He's the associate pastor at Faith. Great guy. He was here the whole time, but he had to leave about five minutes ago to get to another appointment. You just missed him."

Maura wondered how there could be any air left in the room by the time Lainie finished. And she was still pumping away at Maura's arm.

"Well, nice meeting you, Miss Waters." Maura extricated her hand from Lainie's grasp.

She laughed and waved her hand. "I'm just Lainie. So glad we got to meet each other, Maura. And I hope to see you around church. Bye, Pastor Nick."

With a wiggle of her fingers, she was gone.

Nick and Maura looked mutely at each other. Now that it was just the two of them, the house seemed abnormally quiet. "Well," Maura said, "she certainly is . . . perky."

"Yes, she is." Nick scratched the back of his head. "She's only been with us for two months, but she's already doing a great job with the kids."

Maura's chest tightened at the admiration in Nick's voice. "Since when do you have meetings at the house?"

He frowned. "Since I knew you were coming and I wanted to be here when you arrived."

"Oh." His explanation made sense. Besides, whether his meeting was for business or pleasure was none of her business. She'd given up the right to be jealous a long time ago.

The tension in the room nearly suffocated her. She had to say something, anything, to get them on more stable footing. "The place looks nice."

"Thanks." He looked toward the front door in the direction of her car. "Do you have anything to bring in?"

"Tons of stuff. But I can get it later." Maura jiggled the car keys nervously. She stopped and shoved them in her pocket. Did Nick feel as jittery as she did? She couldn't tell if he was just annoyed or nervous too.

He looked around at nothing in particular, then back at her. "Want me to show you where your room is?"

At last, something made her smile. He was nervous. "It's been a long time, but I think I can still remember how to find the spare room."

"Oh, brother." He ran his hand through his hair and down his face. "This day isn't going at all like I planned. I wanted so much to make this simple and easy, but I've got to admit, I don't have a clue how to act."

She appreciated his honesty. It was much easier to deal with the elephant in the room once someone admitted it was there. Of course, she'd rather have a whole herd of elephants to contend with than to be alone with her estranged husband.

"I think we both need something to do right now." She retrieved the keys from her pocket and held them out to him. "There's a suitcase behind the driver's seat. If you could bring that in, I'll get the rest of it later. And while you're doing that, I'll visit the washroom. It's been a long trip."

With a nod Nick took the keys and went out the front door. Now that she was alone, Maura took a closer look at her surroundings. Little had changed since the last time she'd been in this room. The chocolate-brown sofa had faded into a color more closely resembling coffee laced with heavy cream, and the recliner she'd come to think of as "Nick's chair" was just this side of threadbare. But the same battered oak table with the mismatched chairs stood on a brightly colored braided rag rug in the small dining area. The paintings on the walls were the same, as were the curtains that hung at the front windows. All the hand-me-downs they'd been given by well-meaning parishioners still filled the house.

When Maura had learned that Nick's new assignment came with a parsonage, she'd been thrilled. What a blessing to be able to start their married life in their own home. She'd spent hours dreaming of what it would look like, planning how she would pick out each piece of furniture with care, each accessory and knick-knack, creating a home they'd both love. But when they'd arrived, she'd been surprised to find the house completely furnished in what she now thought of as "early American garage sale."

Nick had never let her replace any of it for fear they'd hurt someone's feelings.

"Instead of seeing all this stuff as castoffs, look at it this way," he'd said. "These folks went through their homes and chose family pieces to share with us. What if someone comes over and finds out we got rid of Uncle Joe's recliner? That wouldn't be a good start, would it?"

The members of the congregation had gone out of their way to make them feel welcome. Still, Maura hadn't been able to shake the feeling that she was living in someone else's house.

She looked up at the picture hanging over the fireplace and grimaced. It was a dark, heavy oil painting of three old men in britches and waistcoats, sitting around a rough wood table, holding up what looked to be beer steins. Not only was it a questionable donation to the home of a pastor, it was downright ugly. And it was too heavy to move. She knew because she'd tried.

How could she stand living there again, surrounded by more reminders of how nothing turned out the way she'd hoped?

Maura went into the bathroom, washed her hands, and patted her cheeks with the cool water. Six years ago, she'd come to this house as a newly married woman, excited about the life ahead of her. Now, the face reflected in the mirror was that of a woman hardened by disappointment and loss.

"You can do this," she said to herself. "It's only furniture. No big deal. Just focus on the job you've got to do."

She left the bathroom and collided with Nick in the hall. Her palm braced against his chest just as he grabbed her arms to keep her from falling. The heat from his hands burned through her sleeves and up to her neck. Slowly, she raised her eyes, moving from the middle of his shirt to the open V at the base of his throat to his chin with its sprinkling of light stubble to his lips. And that's where her eyes screeched to a halt. It had been a long time since she'd been this close to his lips.

"Sorry." He pushed her away gently, making sure she was steady before he let go. "I just put your bag in the room."

Maura took a step back, pressing as close to the wall as possible. "Thanks. I appreciate the help."

He smiled. "No problem. You sure you don't want me to get the rest of it?"

"It can wait," she said with a shake of her head.

Nick nodded and looked away again. Yes, this would certainly take some getting used to.

"Why don't we—"

"What are you—"

They both spoke at once, then snapped their mouths shut. Finally, Maura said, "Why don't we move out of the hall, hmm?"

Nick nodded, and they went back into the living room. "So, how was the trip?"

She sighed. "Long. And a little disappointing."

"How so?"

Why had she gone and said that? She could have kept it to herself, and he would have been none the wiser.

"I stopped to see some of the roadside attractions."

The corners of his mouth turned up ever so slightly, stopping just short of a full-blown grin. "I guess that means they didn't live up to your expectations."

"Not even close. You know that big sign for the *genuine* unicorn?"

"Yeah."

"It was a poor little goat with a horn grafted onto his forehead."

Nick lost the battle to keep a straight face. "You didn't expect to see a real one, did you?"

Maura rolled her eyes. "Of course not. But if you paint a picture of a beautiful, horse-like unicorn on your sign, your fake unicorn should at least resemble a horse."

"Good point." He paused, as if debating whether or not to ask the next question. "What about the gopher? Did you stop to see that?"

Now Maura grinned. When they'd made the trip together he'd acted like none of it interested him. It was nice to know he'd been a little curious after all. "Yes, I did. It actually was a three-ton gopher . . . carved out of solid rock. At least that sign was honest—misleading, but honest."

Nick laughed, and she joined with him. Electricity buzzed through the air, tying them together, jerking Maura up short. Why was it so easy to fall into this camaraderie? How could she forget, even for a little while, all the reasons she had for leaving him? Reasons that extended far beyond his spending too much time away from home. Reasons he didn't even know about.

This couldn't happen. Nick had his life, and she had hers. This joint life they'd been forced into was only temporary. Even though they were still legally married, they would never be together in that way again. If she forgot their past, she was asking for more pain.

"What are your plans for today?"

"I should be unpacking," she said, "but that's the last thing I want to do right now." She thought of unpacking the boxes and putting her stuff away in the closet and the dresser, acting as though she belonged in this house. It was something she'd put off as long as she could. "Honestly, I'm itching to work on the theatre."

"So you're heading over there?"

Maura shook her head. "I want to walk around, stretch my legs. I need to get the lay of the land. I know nothing changes much in Granger, but I noticed on the welcome-to-town sign that the population's had a bit of a spike, so something must be different."

Nick cocked his head to one side. "You have no idea, do you?"

"About what?"

This brought out a full-blown smile. "Wow, are you in for a surprise. If you really want to get the big picture, it would be better to drive."

Maura groaned. Her body would revolt if she forced it back into the car.

Nick laughed. "Yeah, I'll bet more driving sounds lousy right now. What if I do the driving and show you the major changes?"

Maura hesitated. It was natural for Nick to want to help. After all, that's what he did for a living. But getting too comfortable with him would only lead to trouble. "You know, that's a sweet offer, but I don't want to put you out."

"The way I see it, it's kind of my responsibility. After all, I have just as much at stake as you do."

"Is that so? How do you figure?"

Nick crossed his arms, shifting his weight to the back of one foot. "Well, if you don't get that theatre in shape, we won't be able to have the church program there. And if that doesn't happen, the church won't get the donation. So it's in my best interest to see you have all the background information you need."

Her spirits sank just a little as she realized he was right. She might as well face facts. No matter how hard she tried to avoid it, the two of them were stuck with each other for six months.

"Okay, you win."

For such a practical man, sometimes Nick was way too impulsive, like offering to drive Maura around. If he had thought it through, he would have realized it was a big mistake. The more time they spent alone together and the more interaction they had, the harder it would be to keep his feelings bottled up. He was leaving himself wide open for more pain.

As they drove down Main Street, he pointed out new businesses, some brand new and others that had taken the place of closed establishments. The first time the two of them had driven down this road, they'd been a happily married couple, exploring their new hometown. Nick had been so excited about the prospect of coming on as an associate and being mentored by Pastor Wesson that everything seemed quaint and full of potential. Maura, on the other hand, kept expressing wonder at the smallness of the town. When she had asked where the Starbuck's was, he should have realized everything wasn't going to be as perfect as he expected.

"What's that?"

Maura pointed at one of the shops across the street. Its bold blue and yellow sign proclaimed The Dot Spot, making it stand out sandwiched between Mabel's Beauty Emporium and The Wee One's Shoe Shack.

"That's your first surprise. Believe it or not, The Dot Spot is Granger's first Internet café."

"You're joking." Her head whipped around for another look. "I thought for sure it was a dry cleaner or something."

"Nope, it's an honest to goodness designer-coffee-and-internet-hookup spot."

"I'll bet the boys at the phone company had a great time wiring that up."

Nick shook his head. "They don't have any dial-up connections."

Maura hesitated. "You mean . . ."

"Yep, it's all high speed and Wi-Fi," Nick finished for her. "Technology has come to Granger."

He glanced over at Maura, who stared out the front window. She had never liked living in Granger. Nick knew the town felt too small and backward to her. She'd said it hadn't changed in a hundred years and wouldn't change in another hundred. How must she feel now to discover she'd been wrong?

They kept driving, and he pointed out other progressive improvements. She simply nodded and muttered the occasional, "Hmm."

When they neared the edge of the commercial district, he pointed off to the right. "You already know what's in that direction. That's the older residential section of Granger. It's pretty much the same as when you were here."

"The *older* section?" she asked. "You mean there's a newer one?"

"Oh, yeah. Boy, are you in for a surprise."

He took a left, went around a corner, and they were immediately greeted by a beautiful tree-lined street full of newer homes. Nick visited members of his congregation in this area regularly, but the sight of all this new growth occasionally still took him by surprise. He could only imagine how Maura must feel.

Beside him, she swung her head from side to side, trying to take in all the houses with their neatly manicured lawns and paved driveways. "When did all this happen?"

"The construction started about three years ago, and phase two was completed about six months ago, so—"

"*Phase two?* How many phases are there?"

Nick held back a grin. "Right now the Granger Commission for Urban Growth has given the go-ahead for phase three, but—"

"Urban growth? Granger actually has a commission that's *encouraging* change and growth now?" If her voice got any higher, she'd attract every dog in the neighborhood.

Poor Maura. She was having a harder time processing the information than he'd expected. "I think we've driven around enough for one day. Why don't we get some coffee and go sit in the park. I'll explain it all to you."

She sat back in her seat, closed her eyes, and nodded. "That's the first thing you've said that's made any sense since we got in the car."

4

What would you like?" Nick asked.

He might as well have asked her to recite the periodic table. "Whatever you're having."

She was gawking. It was rude. But she couldn't stop.

As Nick approached the counter, Maura continued to take in the space around her. The Dot Spot was a clever combination of rural comfort and high-tech convenience. Chunky wooden tables with high-backed chairs were interspersed with overstuffed chairs and couches. Along two walls stood a bar made of what looked like one continuous piece of highly varnished wood. There were some open hookup spaces, but most of them were filled with an eclectic group of people: a professional couple wearing business casual; a few teenage boys sporting various piercings, one of which had a skateboard propped up against his chair; and a fellow who in his overalls and straw hat looked like he'd just come in off the farm. They all shared the space together, drinking coffee and hunched over laptops.

It wasn't an amazing site in and of itself. In fact, with the exception of the woodsy theme, it reminded her of most of the coffee shops she'd ever been to in San Diego. And that was the amazing thing, because she wasn't in San Diego anymore. She was in Granger.

"Here you go."

Nick held out a tall cup. The rich aroma wafted gently under her nose. "Thanks."

She looked around for a place to sit. A few people had already raised their hands in greeting. If they stayed here, Nick would be swarmed, and they'd never be able to talk.

As if reading her mind, Nick motioned to the door. "Why don't we walk to the park."

Maura sipped her tall cup of coffee, only vaguely aware of the mingled tastes of vanilla, nutmeg, and brown sugar. Neither spoke as they strolled across the street and found a bench. Nick was probably giving her time to process all the new information she'd received that day. In contrast Maura's brain had gone on tilt.

Finally, she asked Nick the only question that came to mind. "What happened to Granger?"

He hung one elbow on the back of the bench and angled toward her. "Actually, it's what happened to Beaver Falls that caused all the changes here."

Beaver Falls? She was more confused than ever. Beaver Falls was thirty miles away and almost as stuck in its ways as Granger. How could anything that happened there have brought about all the changes she'd seen?

Nick didn't wait for her to respond. "About four years ago, a small company called Apex Computers relocated to Beaver Falls."

Maura shook her head. "I've never heard of them."

"Neither had anyone else, which was part of their problem. The other part was they were based in northern California in Silicon Valley. At that time real estate prices were at their peak, so even leasing a business facility cost them a fortune.

Anyhow, they did some creative thinking and decided to move their whole operation out to the country, where the pace is slower, the sky is bluer—"

"And the land is cheaper," she said.

Nick nodded. "Exactly. At the same time they changed their name, came up with a catchy marketing campaign, and the company took off."

It finally clicked in Maura's head. "Beaver Computers." She'd seen the commercials with Bucky, the big-toothed animated beaver and their slogan *Beavers Build It Better*. It was corny but cute and odd enough to catch a person's attention. More important, the company backed up their marketing with an excellent product. She owned a Beaver laptop herself. "I see their advertising everywhere, but I had no idea they were based out here."

"The company tripled their revenue in the last few years, which meant they increased their workforce. As new employees moved to the area, housing prices in Beaver Falls went up. Now we're getting the overflow from all the Beaver employees who don't mind commuting if it means paying less for a house. And thanks to their success, a few other major corporations are considering a move into the area." Nick drained his coffee and threw the empty cup into a nearby trash can. "So you see, things do change."

"Yes, they do."

Maura looked around them. There was more traffic on the street, new stores here and there, but Granger still looked like a small town. When she lived here, she had wished for something different, something more. But now, she found herself hoping that Granger didn't lose what made it special.

That was a surprise. When had she ever thought anything about this town was special?

"So now what?" Nick asked.

"Now I need to get to work."

An hour later, Maura sat in the Granger Public Library, surrounded by business books. She'd asked Nick to drop her there so she could do research, but more than that she just wanted a quiet place to gather her thoughts and time to sketch out a plan for the theatre.

Her mind kept returning to the same question: if she hadn't left Granger when she did, would her life have turned out differently? Beaver Computers relocated a few years after she took off. If she'd known the town would be growing, and it really would be changing, would she have stayed?

The answer came to her with a rush. No.

No matter how much Granger had grown, it didn't change the fact that Nick's first love was the church and all his parishioners. The town's growth spurt had probably made that situation worse, since there were so many new souls to worry about. And nothing could make up for what she lost or erase the heartache that finally spurred her to leave Nick.

"Maura Shepherd?"

A familiar voice pulled her from her reverie. She opened her mouth to correct the person—*it's Sullivan, not Shepherd*—when she recognized an old friend.

"Rachel?"

Her hips were a little bit wider than the last time Maura had seen her, and her hair was a whole lot redder, but she would have recognized Rachel Nelson anywhere. Rachel was the closest friend she'd had in Granger and one of the few people who knew the whole truth about what had happened between her and Nick. Maura's immediate joy at seeing Rachel was tempered with shame for the way she'd handled her exit from town.

But Rachel wasn't the type to hold a grudge. With a grin as wide as Lake Erie, she grabbed Maura's hands, hauled her to her feet, and engulfed her in a bear hug. "I heard you were coming back. I can't tell you how good it is to see you!"

Maura hugged her back, feeling a surge of genuine happiness for the first time in weeks. "It's good to see you too."

Mrs. Phipps, the head librarian, walked up to them. A serious woman who wore serious clothes and her hair in a seriously severe bun, she'd been a fixture in the library for as long as anyone could remember. She was also a strict enforcer of the rules of library conduct, particularly the one about never talking above a stage whisper within its hallowed halls. Putting her finger to her lips, she gave Rachel and Maura a hearty "shush" before continuing on her way back to the information desk. The reprimand only served to send the two friends into fits of giggles.

Rachel composed herself, stepping back to give Maura a good once-over. "My, my," Rachel said softly, "you don't look a bit different since the last time I saw you. What's it been, five years?"

"A little over six." Maura tucked a stray piece of hair behind her ear. "Rachel, I owe you an apology. I'm so sorry I didn't tell you what I was doing. I . . ."

Rachel held up her hand. "It's done and over with. One day, if you want, we can have a long talk about it, but today is not that day."

She casually motioned with her head toward the front desk where Mrs. Phipps held court. It was a well-known fact that, while the woman frowned on people talking in the library, she had no qualms about eavesdropping on conversations when they were audible, as it gave her lots of new information to share during her weekly wash and set at Mabel's.

"What I really want," Rachel continued, "is to get the whole scoop on why you're back now."

Maura laughed. "I'm surprised you haven't already heard it through the grapevine."

"Just bits and pieces. I know it has something to do with Miss Hattie's will. But I need to know the facts."

"It's a long story," Maura cautioned.

"I've got time." Rachel plunked herself down in the seat on the other side of the table.

Maura sat down and in hushed, library-appropriate tones told Rachel everything. She only intended to hit the high points, but the more she talked, the more details she filled in. With each piece of information she shared, her spirit lightened a little more.

The last few years hadn't been easy. When Maura left Granger and returned home to California, she'd found that her father wasn't doing nearly as well as he'd claimed. His health was failing, and it had started to affect his work at the coffee shop. Soon, not only had Maura taken over the day-to-day operations of Sullivan's, she'd also become her father's primary caregiver. There had been little time for anything other than work and Da. She'd done it without complaining, glad to be able to fill her days with something other than feelings of regret. Not until now did she realize how much she'd missed having a close friend to share with.

"So that's it," Maura said when she finished the saga. "And now here I am, sitting in the library, trying to make sense out of it all."

Rachel laughed and shook her head. "That Miss Hattie sure was a spunky old gal, right up until the end. She knew exactly what bait to dangle in front of you and Pastor Nick to get you two back together."

Maura bristled. "We're not getting back together."

"Maybe not," Rachel shrugged. "But you are living together again. And you've got to work together to pull this off. Who knows where all that close proximity might lead?"

"It won't lead to anything other than me getting the theatre up and running and him getting a nice donation for his precious church. As soon as the six months are up, I'm moving out of the parsonage, and we never have to see each other again."

"Come on, Maura. Would it be so bad if something did spark between you two? You've got to still have feelings for him to be so upset by this situation. I know for a fact he never stopped loving you."

"How can you know that?" Maura hated herself for asking, but as much as she acted like she didn't care, she really wanted to know.

"He was a mess when you left. He called all over looking for you." Rachel leaned closer. "He even showed up at my doorstep, wanting to know if I could tell him anything."

Maura's face went cold. "What did you say?"

She frowned. "Nothing. I wanted to tell him about, well, you know . . . but I didn't. It wasn't my place. I just said I didn't know you were leaving, which was the truth. Maura, if you'd seen him . . . I've never seen anyone so devastated in my life."

Maura looked down at her left hand, where she used to wear her wedding ring. "I've been gone for a long time," she said slowly. "Not once did he call my father or come looking for me. He couldn't have missed me that much."

"I don't know why he didn't go after you, but I know he chose to stay married to you, even though you left. I'll bet you didn't know, but the church board met about a year after you'd gone to discuss the situation. At that point it was pretty obvious you weren't coming back. They decided that since you abandoned Pastor Nick, he had legitimate grounds to divorce you."

"What?" Maura was shocked they would even suggest such a thing.

"I know. I couldn't believe it when I found out. I guess they figured they couldn't hold your actions against him so they were trying to be decent . . . give him an out so he could go on with his life but not lose his job."

"Or maybe they just wanted him to remarry so there'd be a pastor's wife to oversee the Thursday morning women's devotion group." She hated the tone of sarcasm that crept into her voice. After all these years, she should be over it.

"Maybe. I don't know what their motivation was. All I know is that Nick turned them down. Why would he have done that if he didn't still love you?"

Maura didn't have an answer. Nick was nothing if not principled. The fact that he'd made a vow to be united with Maura "till death parts us" was probably enough to keep him married to her. On the other hand, if he was shown proof that his marriage was over and could be made null and void in the eyes of God and the church council, wouldn't he have jumped at that? That is, if he wanted to get out.

But Maura didn't want to think about that now. It was old business, and she had new, more pressing matters in front of her. "I have no way of knowing what Nick was thinking," she finally told Rachel. "What I do know is that I've got a run-down old theatre that needs to be overhauled, and I have to figure out how to make it a viable enterprise."

Rachel took the hint. "Seems to me, first you need to decide exactly what purpose you want it to serve."

Maura pursed her lips. "That's a good point. I guess I haven't thought about it as anything other than a theatre for live productions."

"Just because that's what it was doesn't mean that's what it always has to be. A leopard may not be able to change its spots, but a building sure can." Rachel winked at her.

Maura laughed, enjoying how easily they'd slipped back on the old shoe of familiarity. "Okay, since you're so full of good ideas, what are some other uses for the space?"

Rachel leaned back in her chair, eyes cast at the ceiling. "Well, you could put in a screen and turn it into a movie theater. Or you could turn it into a type of convention center . . . a place to have meetings and such. Or you could put in tables and make it a dinner theatre."

"Or I could do it all."

Rachel narrowed her eyes. "Just how many buildings do you think you inherited?"

"No, no, listen. I could do it all in one building." Maura felt her cheeks flush with excitement. "One of the conditions of the will is that we put on at least one church performance, so we have to keep the live theatre aspect, which I want to do anyway. But I don't think that alone will bring in enough revenue. If I installed a retractable screen, we could also have special movie viewings. And with the new businesses that are thinking of moving this way, we could certainly rent it out for corporate meetings."

"What about dinner theatre?"

Maura chewed on her lower lip. "Okay, that would be a lot harder. I don't think there are any cooking facilities in the building, and to install a professional kitchen would be too expensive. But we could probably offer some kind of dinner-and-a-show package in conjunction with one of the restaurants in town."

"That's a great idea." Rachel nodded, catching Maura's enthusiasm. "I envy you, Maura."

Was she serious? "Me? Why?"

"Because you've got this great opportunity to make something out of practically nothing. You're reinventing your life. What I wouldn't give for a chance like that."

Rachel's wistful tone surprised Maura. From where she sat, Rachel had the perfect life: a great husband, two kids, the house with an actual white picket fence. What more could she want?

"Are you looking to reinvent yourself?"

Rachel's eyes widened. "No, not really. I guess that's not the right word. I love my life, it's just . . ."

"Just what?" Maura prodded.

Rachel hesitated before plunging in. "I've been a full-time housewife and mom since I was eighteen. Don't get me wrong. I love my family, but the kids don't need me nearly as much as they used to. I have a lot of extra time on my hands. Lately, I've been thinking about what comes next. You know, when the nest is empty and it's just Derrick and me."

Maura nodded, a plan already percolating in her brain. "I completely get what you're saying. And, you're right. This theatre is a great opportunity for me. But you know I can't pull it off by myself. I'll need some good people to work with." She paused. "Are you interested?"

Rachel looked at her cautiously. "Why? Are you making me an offer?"

"I couldn't pay you much . . . in fact, I can't actually pay you anything until we start bringing in some revenue." Maura stopped, embarrassed that she'd suggested Rachel work for free. "Never mind, it's a dumb idea. Just forget I said anything."

"Whoa, there!" Rachel waved her hands back and forth in front of Maura. "You just let me decide whether or not it's a dumb idea. Besides, you're offering me twice as much as I'm making now."

"How do you figure?"

"Twice as much of nothing is nothing," Rachel said with a grin. "I don't know if you've heard, but people in my job category don't even make minimum wage. Besides, now you've got me all revved up about the idea of reviving the Music Box."

Maura's heart constricted as she looked across the table. Not all of her experiences in Granger had been bad. Rachel was a sincere, true friend, who had been there for her when she was at her lowest. Despite the fact that Maura had abandoned the friendship, Rachel was gracious enough to let them pick up like nothing had happened. Working with her now would definitely be a good thing. She might even call it an answer to prayer, if she prayed anymore.

She was about to say something profound when her stomach grumbled loudly, making both of the woman laugh. Maura glanced down at her watch. "Good grief, it's later than I thought. You probably need to get back home."

Rachel shook her head. "Nope, everybody's got other plans tonight. Becca's at a friend's house, and from there she's going to chorus practice; Ben's away at football camp, and Derrick has a church board meeting. We're spread out all over, which proves my point. You know, I think this is what Pastor Nick might call a divine appointment."

Maura let Rachel's last statement slide. Rachel didn't need to know Maura no longer shared Nick's belief that God was involved in all areas of a person's life. Maura thought of God as more of a passive observer. Otherwise, her life would have turned out much differently.

Maura cleared her throat, eager to steer the conversation in a different direction. "Why don't you and I go get dinner and do some more brainstorming?"

"Great idea. I'll just leave a message for Derrick in case he gets home before I do." Rachel pulled her cell phone from her purse.

"Hm—hm." Mrs. Phipps's eyes narrowed as she cast a laser look toward Rachel. Apparently, using cell phones in the library was a cardinal sin, deemed even worse than mere conversation.

Rachel flipped the phone shut and stuffed it back in her purse. "Maybe I'll call him from outside," she whispered loudly.

Maura scooped up the books she'd already checked out, and they headed for the door. She couldn't believe how everything was coming together. It was almost as if somebody had sent Rachel into the library so they could run into each other. Maura shook her head sharply. What was she thinking? It was coincidence, pure and simple. A happy, fortunate coincidence. A few more of those, and this project might turn out all right after all.

5

Maura was still so excited after her first unofficial business meeting with Rachel that she almost didn't notice Nick when she walked into the house. The sounds from the kitchen got her attention, and that's where she found him, putting away what looked like dinner leftovers. She inhaled deeply. Something sure smelled good. Was that roast beef? She didn't see any evidence of it, but her nose wouldn't lie to her.

"Hey, when did you learn how to cook?" She cringed as soon as the words were out of her mouth. *What do you think, stupid, he stopped eating after you left him?*

Nick had the good grace not to point that out. He turned from the sink, wiping his hands on a dish towel. "Surprising, I know, but I can kind of find my way around the kitchen. Actually, roast is one of the easier meals to make."

Maura thought back to her conversation with Rachel. "I'm surprised you're home. Didn't you have to be at the church board meeting tonight?"

"I told them I couldn't be there." Nick shrugged. "Since this is your first night here, well, I wanted to . . ." His voice trailed off and he tossed the dish towel on the counter. "I just wanted to be around."

This was a first. He'd skipped a meeting for her. And he'd cooked dinner. She dropped her purse on the dining table and noticed it was set with her mother's china. Her heart jumped.

Da had given the set to them as a wedding present. When she left Nick, she'd been so upset that she hardly took anything. She left the dishes behind, never expecting to see them again. Now, running a finger gently around the rim of a plate, she smiled. Nick used to be afraid to touch them because he'd accidentally broken one of the tea cups. Yet, he'd brought them out today. "You kept the set."

He looked shocked that she'd considered anything else. "Of course. I know how much it means to you. I figured someday you'd send for it, or come back to get it." He shook his head. "Of course, I never figured this was how you'd end up coming back."

He'd gone to so much trouble. Not just preparing the meal and setting the table, but he'd cleared his calendar for the evening. It warmed her down to her toes. "Nick, I'm sorry. I had no idea you'd done all this. If I had, I would have come . . . back." She'd almost called it *home*. But she couldn't. She couldn't let herself start thinking about this as home, no matter how good it smelled, or how irresistible Nick looked with his sleeves rolled up and water spots all over the front of his shirt.

"No big deal. I had to eat, anyway. And now we've got leftovers." He dismissed her concerns with a raise of one shoulder, as though the situation didn't bother him. But Maura could hear the twinge of disappointment in his voice. "So, have you eaten already?"

She nodded. "I ran into Rachel Nelson at the library. We ended up having dinner."

His smile became genuine. "That's great. I'm glad you're reconnecting with old friends."

Friend, she thought. There wasn't anyone else she'd connected with during her short residence in Granger. She'd tried to work with people: Bettie Schwaab on the Thursday morning Bible study, Lena Tyler on the Vacation Bible School planning committee, Stu Pierson on the hospital visitation team, to name a few. She'd tried and failed to work with so many people. The experiences had not bound her in friendship to a single person. But Nick wouldn't know that. He'd thought she was getting along great with everyone, and she'd let him believe it. If he still believed it, there was no need to set him straight now.

"Yeah, it was fun catching up with her. But it was so much more than that. We started talking about the theatre and—"

Nick raised his hand like a traffic cop bringing her to a halt. "Wait. This sounds interesting. Why don't we sit down, have some pie, and you can fill me in? Unless you've already had dessert too."

"No, we skipped dessert." She saw the pie sitting on the counter, covered in aluminum foil. "What kind is it?"

"Cherry. Your favorite. And yes," he said before she could ask, "we do have vanilla ice cream."

Once more, Maura felt off balance. This was the same man who frequently forgot to call home to say he'd be missing dinner. Who left the house before the sun rose and often didn't return until close to midnight. Who expected her to jump into every kind of service project with the same abandon he did. Yet here he was, not only remembering her favorite pie, but that she liked it a la mode. This must be what Alice felt like when she went through the looking glass. Everything upside down and not as it used to be.

Maura pushed her confused thoughts aside and concentrated on the present moment. She'd felt completely full and satisfied after finishing dinner with Rachel, but now her stomach called out. Apparently, there was always room for pie.

She took off her jacket and draped it across the back of a chair. "Okay, you sold me. You dish it up, and I'll clear off the table."

Nick smiled and moved to the counter. Still feeling flustered, Maura turned to the table and collected the clean silver, leaving out the spoons so they could use them for dessert. As Nick spooned the pie and ice cream into chunky cereal bowls, she carefully stacked the good china. Without even thinking, she carried the plates to the opposite end of the kitchen and opened the cupboard next to the refrigerator. Sure enough, he still kept the set there. It was oddly comforting that, so far, everything was the same as she remembered.

Everything except for Nick himself. It was eight o'clock on a week night, and there he stood, serving up pie. When they had first lived together in Granger, there was always something to do, some meeting or emergency to attend to, some reason for Nick to run off or not come home until late. Most nights, she'd been alone in the house. When he did stay home, he was so preoccupied with his next sermon or Bible study that she may as well have been alone. Now he wanted to sit, eat pie, and talk about her day. Amazing.

"All set."

Maura turned to see that not only had Nick put the pie on the table, he'd filled glasses of ice water for both of them. He sat down and motioned for her to join him, then dug into his dessert, giving a moan of pleasure at the first bite.

"You're pretty satisfied with your cooking," Maura said as she sat across the table.

He shook his head. "I can't take credit for the pie. Baking is not a skill I've been able to pick up. Thankfully, the seniors group took me on as one of their service projects. They bless me with something sweet once a week."

Of course. The congregation loved Nick, no doubt about that. And they loved feeding him. From the moment Nick and Maura first arrived in Granger, the Ladies' Auxiliary had barraged the couple with covered dishes. The first week alone they'd received so many casseroles Maura had to start packing them into the freezer. Just the thought made her stomach roll. If she never saw another casserole again it would be too soon.

Turning her thoughts back to dessert, she took a bite of the pie. The mixture of tart cherries and smooth vanilla ice cream almost pulled a moan out of her too. Instead, she just smiled. "It's very good."

"So," he said, leaning forward, "tell me about your wonderful day."

In between bites she told him how she'd run into Rachel and the ideas they'd come up with. The more she talked, the more excited she became, until she'd forgotten about her dessert altogether. Nick didn't interrupt as she went on about her plans. He just listened attentively and scraped his bowl clean.

"So, what do you think?" she asked when she'd run out of news to tell him.

"I think it's incredible. You've got a lot of great ideas, and it's wonderful that you've already got someone on board to work with. Rachel's a good woman."

Nick's casual statement set off warning bells in Maura's head. Rachel's a good woman, the kind who supports her husband and looks after her children. The kind who would never abandon her family. The kind you can depend on. *Not at all like you.*

She pressed her lips together tightly and looked down at her bowl. What was left of the pie had become a congealed mess of soggy crust and melted ice cream. It wasn't nearly so appetizing now. She stood up and took their bowls to the sink to rinse them out.

Get a grip, she scolded herself. *Rachel is a good woman. And you're doing the best you can.*

"It's not just Rachel," she said over her shoulder. "Her husband Derrick's a CPA. Of course, you already know that. Anyway, I'll definitely need financial and tax advice, so I'm going to meet with him later this week."

As if on autopilot, she loaded the dishes in the dishwasher. She washed her hands, dried them on a towel hanging from the oven handle, and turned back to face Nick. An odd expression passed over his face. Was it yearning, or maybe sadness? Whatever it was, it was gone nearly as fast as it came.

"Hiring Derrick is a good strategic move," he said. "Not only will he be a great advisor, but it will give you an ally on the church council."

She leaned back against the sink and crossed her arms. "Why do I need an ally on the church council?"

Nick cocked his head to one side, his mouth twisting in amusement. "In order to carry out the conditions of the will, you're going to have to meet with them to coordinate having a church function at the theatre."

A moment of panic gripped Maura. She'd never attended a council meeting before, but she'd had dealings with the council members. Each one had their own idea of what a pastor's wife should be like, and Maura hadn't been able to live up to any of them. The last thing she wanted to do was meet them as a group. "Is it absolutely necessary for me to meet with the council?"

"I think so." Nick was all business now. "There's a certain chain of command at a church. In order to organize your program, you'll have to meet with the heads of the different areas of ministry, and the best way to do that is to attend a council meeting."

Maura shook her head. "I have no desire to put myself under the scrutiny of the council again. In fact, if Miss Hattie hadn't made this ridiculous performance provision, I wouldn't set foot in that church again. Why can't I just work out all the details with you?"

She never should have said that. Nick's eyes grew hard. "Yes, avoidance would be so much easier for you." An unfamiliar tone of sarcasm crept into his voice. "Unfortunately, we don't always get to do things the easy way. Maybe you should—"

He stopped in mid-sentence and pulled his cell phone from its belt clip. He must have had it on vibrate because he looked at the display on the front and frowned. "I've got to take this." He flipped the phone open as he headed out of the kitchen. "Hello. Hold on a second." He stopped in the doorway and turned back to Maura. "I'll arrange a special council meeting next week to address this will business. If I were you, I'd spend some time getting ready." He did an about-face, put the phone back to his ear, and resumed his conversation with the person on the other end. His voice grew fainter as he walked to his study. The door closed with a dull thud, leaving Maura standing in the silence.

Well, that was it. It had taken longer than it used to, but this night ended up just like so many others had, with Nick dismissing her to take care of someone else. Maura was blind-sided by the disappointment lodged in her heart.

She stood alone in the kitchen, her arms still wrapped around her sides. She'd been foolish to forget for even a moment that she was an outsider here. Yes, Nick had made dinner and served her dessert, but he would have done that for anybody. Nick took care of people, plain and simple. But as soon as someone else needed him, he was off to see to their needs.

The congregation always came first. If she'd understood that before, when they first moved to Granger, the outcome might have been different.

There was no use in looking back. She understood it now. And she wouldn't soon forget it.

—∞∞—

"How did it go?"

Nick sat in his desk chair, his foot crossed over one knee, his cell phone to his ear. On the other end, his Associate Pastor, Chris Zeeble, reported the status of the church council meeting.

"Like you probably expected," Chris answered. "Most of the council was surprised you weren't at the meeting. I'd say a few of them were just this side of miffed."

Nick shook his head. He hadn't missed a meeting once since he was installed. Evidently, some people did expect perfection.

"No big surprise there. Anything else I should know about?"

Chris went down the list of old news items that had been addressed. Bids were being taken for a new groundskeeper. The music director had submitted her plans for a Christmas cantata. Items from the church nursery team, the kitchen committee, and the new youth leader had been voted on and approved.

"Wait a minute," Nick cut in. "They approved Lainie's youth ministry plan? Just like that?"

There'd been so much opposition to hiring the young woman as the youth director that Nick had expected a battle every time she proposed a new program. Maybe he hadn't given the council members enough credit.

"They didn't spend much time talking about Lainie's plan," Chris answered. "Probably because they wanted to move on to new business."

Nick brought his foot down hard and stiffened in his chair. Jumping into new business when the Senior Pastor wasn't present could only mean one thing: the topic was the Senior Pastor himself.

"This is about Maura, isn't it?"

Chris hesitated before answering. "Yes. More specifically, the fact that you and Maura are living together. Not the whole council," he was quick to add, "but several vocal members seem to feel you're setting a bad example."

A bad example? By living with his wife? "Did somebody think to bring up the fact that Maura and I are still married?"

"Yes, absolutely. But the sticking point is that she left you, and you've been separated for so long. Some of them seem to think it negates the whole 'till death do us part' line in the ceremony."

Nick didn't trust himself to speak. So he waited. And counted.

"Are you still there?" Chris's voice cut into the silence.

"Yes," he answered curtly. "I was just counting to ten. Seems I've been doing that a lot lately." Nick sighed. *Help me, Lord. You're the only one who can straighten out this mess.* "If I try to look at this from an outsider's perspective, I guess I can see where they might have some concerns." Actually, he couldn't, but he was trying.

"They've got to see the situation for what it is. The only reason Maura is living with me, the only reason she even came back in the first place, is because of the will. Miss Hattie meant well, God bless her dear sweet soul, but just because she tried to play matchmaker doesn't mean it will work. I'm helping Maura with the theatre because it's the right thing to do and it will benefit the church. As for our personal involvement, we haven't so much as shaken hands. She's living in this house, but we are *not* living together."

"Do you still love her?"

The younger pastor's question brought him up short. Rising from his chair, he walked across the office to the bookshelf. There, pushed back between two large Bible commentaries, was a framed photo of himself and Maura on their wedding day. They were so happy and hopeful, as if the whole world was open to them. It was like looking at two strangers.

Nick sighed. "How do you stop loving someone? Of course I still love her, but it's different now. You know that old Beatles' song, "All You Need Is Love?" Well, it's a bunch of baloney. Love will only take you so far. There's also sacrifice and commitment and faith and—"

"I get the picture," Chris said, bringing Nick's rambling to a halt. "How's Maura doing in the faith department?"

"Struggling. I'm not even sure she believes God exists anymore. If she does, she doesn't believe He cares about her personally. And I'm partly responsible for that."

"How so?"

"I've had a lot of time to think about what happened between us. I know I made mistakes. I spent almost all of my time doing church work, and I just assumed Maura would want to do the same."

"That's not good, but it doesn't seem big enough to make her lose faith in God."

Nick frowned. No, it didn't. And he didn't think that alone was what upset her enough to leave him. "You're right. There had to be something else. I just don't know what it is. But it shook her foundations, and she hasn't had an easy time since. Her father died a few months ago, and I think that was the final blow."

"So she's become a project for you now."

Nick smiled. Part of the reason he'd wanted an associate pastor was to have someone to confide in. Chris hadn't known him long, but he certainly knew him well. "Yes, I guess you could say that. Her spiritual well-being has to be my first priority."

"I agree. But don't forget about *your* well-being, spiritual and otherwise."

"What do you mean?"

"You're the type of man who puts everybody else first. It's an honorable trait, but if you're not careful, you'll run out of steam. You'll give so much of yourself there will be nothing left for you."

Nick fought back irritation. Wasn't a pastor supposed to sacrifice for his congregation? Wasn't he supposed to be Christ-like? Why was that a problem all of a sudden?

"So what's your point?" he asked Chris.

"Even if you're able to help Maura reconnect with her faith, that doesn't mean she'll want to resume her role as your wife, or even stay in town. For all you know, she may decide to sell the theatre as soon as the property transfers over to her and be on her way. And if that happens, I don't want to see your heart leave town with her."

6

It became clear to Nick that he and Maura needed to set some ground rules when he ran into her the next morning. He left his bedroom, still half asleep, when the door to the bathroom opened and Maura stepped out.

In her bathrobe.

For a moment Nick couldn't process her presence. Maura was in his house. Damp strands of hair curled around her face. A flame of contentment sparked to life deep in his core. She was so beautiful.

She was so appalled. "Nick, I'm sorry. I didn't even realize you were still here. Your door was shut, and I thought . . ." Her words trailed off as she pulled the edges of her robe closer.

Cold reality doused Nick's flame. Yes, Maura was in his house, but he wasn't supposed to be so happy to see her. And he certainly wasn't supposed to be checking her out in her bathrobe.

"No, Maura, it's okay. I'm sorry. I—" He touched his chest. Oops. "I'm not wearing a shirt. Hold on one second."

He ducked back into his room and threw on a T-shirt. When he came back into the hall, it was empty.

"Maura?"

"I'm in here." Her voice called out from behind her closed bedroom door. "I'll be right out."

Rather than wait for her by the door like a vulture, he went to the kitchen and poured two cups of coffee. He was sitting at the table when she walked in. She'd put on jeans and a T-shirt and fastened her still-damp hair at the base of her neck with a big clip.

With a questioning look she pointed at the extra coffee cup.

"I figured we could both use this." He motioned to the chair across from him. "Do you have time to sit?"

"Sure." She sank into the chair and wrapped her hands around the mug. Neither one spoke for a moment. Finally, she laughed. "I guess Miss Hattie didn't stop to think about this house having only one bathroom."

Nick shook his head. He'd been thinking just the opposite. The old gal probably counted on the close quarters to work to her advantage. "It will help if we work out some kind of schedule. But that's not what I wanted to talk to you about."

She took a drink of her coffee, waiting for him to continue.

"I want to apologize for last night."

"Really?" She was so surprised, she nearly dropped her cup.

"Really. I shouldn't have been so hard on you. You do have to deal with the council, but I can understand why you wouldn't want to."

She set the cup down and put her palms flat on the table. "Thanks, Nick. And I'm sorry I missed dinner. If I'd known—"

He held up his hand. "It's okay. You couldn't have known. But you bring up a good point. I think we need to be clear on what we do and don't expect from each other during the next six months."

"I don't expect anything," she said quickly. "You don't have to change your life to accommodate me."

He smiled. That was so far from the truth. His life had changed the minute he pushed the "open" button on that elevator door.

Maura wrinkled her nose. "Maybe that approach is too simplistic. What I mean is we should consider ourselves roommates. We can come and go as we please. We'll take care of our own meals. That kind of thing."

"You're okay with that?"

"Absolutely."

"And what about the morning bathroom situation?"

She snatched up her coffee cup and took a gulp. "You're absolutely right. We need a schedule."

———

Maura felt like a mouse entering a room of hungry cats when she walked into the Faith Community Church conference room. Her instincts told her to turn around and walk out, but before she had the chance a few people stood up to greet her. Derrick Nelson, who several days earlier had agreed to be her accountant and financial advisor, met her with a firm handshake and an encouraging pat on the back. Next came Chris, the associate pastor, and Lainie, the youth director, both of whom surprised her with warm hugs. The rest of the council members, not bothering to leave their chairs, simply nodded or said a curt "Hello."

"Pastor Nick will be with us in a moment," Chris said, "and then we can get started."

Maura sat at the end of the long conference room table and busied herself by reading the framed posters adorning the walls. Each one was done in bright colors and showcased a

Bible verse. One particularly exuberant poster, quoting Psalm 35:9, exclaimed "Then my soul will rejoice in the Lord, and delight in His salvation!" Ironically, Oren Thacker, head of the church council and the man sitting in front of the poster, looked like he was neither rejoicing nor delighted.

And he wasn't the only one. For people who were supposed to be full of the "joy of the Lord" a lot of them sure seemed cross.

Maura knew many of these people from her previous life in Granger. Her memories of them, Oren in particular, were that they'd welcomed her effusively and fawned over her until discovering she wasn't exactly the kind of pastor's wife they'd envisioned. The harder she tried to fit into their mold, the more it squeezed, until she burst out of their expectations all together. When she left Granger, she never thought she'd see any of these people again. Judging from their faces, they would have been perfectly happy with that.

The door opened and Maura said a silent thank you when she saw Nick standing there. The sooner they got started, the sooner she'd be out from under the microscope.

"Sorry I'm late," Nick said as he entered the room. He shut the door behind him and took the empty seat next to Maura. Smiling, he looked around the table. "How is everyone today?"

Maura smiled back, but before she could respond, Oren spoke up. "If you don't mind, Pastor, I'd like to dispense with the pleasantries and get right to the issues surrounding Miss Hattie's will. Since we had to convene for this special meeting, there's some church business I'd like to address. That is, after we've put that other matter behind us."

Maura's cheeks grew hot as the man pinned her with his glare. It was quite clear he wanted to deal with her and get her out of the way so she wouldn't be privy to any *important* church business. She met Oren's gaze, refusing to look away. She had zero interest in anything else they had to discuss, but she wasn't willing to let this man push her around. Not again.

"Actually, I believe our first order of business is to open with prayer." Nick's voice was firm. He looked around the table as if daring anyone to disagree with him. "Shall we?"

Maura hesitated, then folded her hands together in her lap. She knew the preferred prayer posture at Faith Community was to take the hand of the person sitting next to you. But Maura couldn't do it. She'd feel like a hypocrite, holding hands and acting like they were all friends. A wave of relief washed over her as Nick also chose to forgo the tradition, folding his own hands and bowing his head, inviting the others to do the same.

"Dear Lord, we thank you for this opportunity to meet together to seek your direction for this church and its people. We thank you, Lord, that you have made this a place where all are loved and welcomed, even as you love and welcome us though we are still sinners. Give us ears to hear and hearts to know your will. In Jesus' name we pray, amen."

"Amen." Maura echoed the sentiment with everyone else, surprising herself as she did so. It had been a long time since she'd prayed, or even voiced agreement to a prayer. Some things, she supposed, became so much a part of you that you just did them instinctively.

She glanced over at Nick. His prayer, while definitely heartfelt, had also diffused some of the tension in the room. Many of the folks who had looked so unhappy a few moments before, now seemed slightly sheepish. Even Oren had been affected. And Lainie, who seemed to live in a perpetual state of happiness, was downright giddy.

"Let's begin, shall we?" Nick stood and turned his attention to Oren. "I think it would be fine to start with the matter of

Miss Hattie's will. After all, there's no reason to bore Maura with the rest of our business."

Nick was in full leader-of-the-flock mode now. Maura couldn't help but admire how he took over the meeting. He gave a quick rundown of the provisions in Miss Hattie's will, including the living arrangements at the parsonage, but did so in such a matter-of-fact way that if anyone wanted to make an issue out of it, they didn't have a chance. He made a point to connect with everyone, looking around the room as he spoke and making eye contact with each person. Finally, he got to the part about the theatre and how it needed to be used to host at least one church event.

"After the event is completed and the six-month living arrangement has been satisfied, Maura will receive the deed to the property, and the church will receive a generous donation from Miss Hattie's estate. So you see, by working together, we'll all come out winners. Now, I'd like to turn this over to Maura so she can tell you what she has in mind."

As Nick sat down, every head at the table seemed to turn in her direction in unison. Maura hadn't expected this meeting to be easy, so she'd been especially thorough in her preparation. Over the past week, she and Rachel had outlined everything that needed to be done at the theatre and what it would take to get the place back into working condition. She had facts, figures, even a timeline for the renovation. Even though the church council had no say over what she did with the theatre, she wanted them to know she was serious about the project. Most of the people in the room were business owners themselves and members of the chamber of commerce. As a new business owner in the community, this was Maura's first chance to win them over.

She'd gone over her presentation again and again and felt confident it was sound. But now, with the members of the council looking at her, waiting for her to convince them that she was capable, even worthy, of the undertaking, she began to doubt herself. Was she ready for this? Would any of them even care about her project?

"I can't wait to hear what you've got in mind." Lainie's eager, positive statement broke through Maura's haze.

She looked at the youth leader and gave her a grateful smile. "I'm glad you're excited, because the youth group will play a big part in this."

Maura passed out the information packets she'd put together before the meeting and began to review her plans for the theatre. As she spoke, her own excitement took over, disengaging the tentacles of fear and doubt that tried to choke off her confidence. Finally, she wrapped up the details of all the work that needed to be done to the building. Now came the tough part.

"When it came time to decide what type of joint event we should hold at the theatre, the answer seemed obvious," she said, trying to sound as upbeat as possible. "I'd like to put on a Christmas Gala to be held the Saturday before Christmas."

There was a smattering of murmurs around the table. Tom Anderson, the high school principal and Faith's Sunday school superintendent, raised a finger and spoke. "We've always held the Sunday school Christmas program at the church on the Sunday before Christmas. Frankly, it's tradition, and I don't think anyone would like to see us change that."

"I agree," Maura said. "I don't want to do anything to interfere with the Sunday school program. I'm talking about something completely different. This would be a combination of songs and drama extending beyond the members of Sunday school. More like a revue."

"And who all's going to be in this revue?" Oren asked.

Maura turned to Lainie. "That's where the youth group comes in. I'll bet there's a lot of untapped talent there. Also, we'll let the community know, and see who comes forward. There will be more than enough people who want to get on stage, trust me."

Oren scowled, his eyebrows coming together to form a bushy V between his eyes. "Trust is something you must earn, *Mrs. Shepherd.* I think I speak for the entire council when I say that it will take more than talk and a bunch of pretty charts to earn our trust." He pushed the folder away from him with one finger. "When I see you back this up with action, I might begin to trust you."

He may as well have spit at her. If she had any doubts about the council's feelings for her, Oren had made them perfectly clear. Not only did they mistrust her, but they didn't expect her to follow through with her promises. When she hurt Nick, she hurt the congregation as well. When she walked out on her marriage, the council took it as a personal betrayal. The only way to earn their trust was to prove she meant what she said, no matter what.

The uncomfortable silence was broken by Lainie, once again coming to the rescue. "You can count on the youth group, Maura. And not just to be in the Gala. I've been hoping to find a good service project to get them involved in. We'll help with the renovations too."

"That brings up another very important point." Oren leaned forward in his chair, elbows on the table. "While the restoration of the theatre will certainly benefit the community, the church is in no position to allocate any finances to this project. Is that understood?"

Maura wanted to reply that not only had she not asked for their help, but she wouldn't take it, even if they offered. She didn't want the council involved any more than was absolutely necessary. But her practical side stopped her. The man was so puffed up he looked like his head was ready to pop. No point antagonizing him further. So she simply answered, "Yes."

Oren swung his gaze to Lainie. "Miss Waters, while I'm sure the youth could find better ways of spending their time, their participation will be left to your discretion. But absolutely no money is to be used from the youth fund toward this project. Are we clear?"

"Absolutely." For the first time that day Lainie's tone was less than bubbly.

"Fine." Oren gave a sharp nod. "If there's no more discussion, we can put it to a vote."

"Excuse me, but I have a few questions for Mrs. Shepherd."

Maura turned toward Pastor Chris. "What would you like to know?"

"Mrs. Shepherd, there are some members of the board who are concerned about you and Pastor Nick living together in the parsonage. I was wondering if you could address that."

Something twisted in the pit of Maura's stomach. She didn't know anything about the young pastor, but her first impression upon meeting him was that he would be fair. His question took her completely by surprise. She looked at Nick. It was clear from his expression he hadn't seen it coming, either. And she was almost certain he was counting.

Maura looked back at Chris. She wanted to ask him why he'd brought this subject up. She wanted to tell him to stop calling her Mrs. Shepherd. She wanted to run out of the room. But she knew her only option was to stay calm and answer his question.

"One of the stipulations of the will is that I live in the parsonage during the next six months. Obviously, Miss Hattie watched one soap opera too many and decided to play matchmaker from beyond the grave." Her nervous laughter bounced weakly against the walls of the hushed room. Apparently, no one else got the joke. Maura rushed on. "So, yes, I am living at the parsonage. I sleep in the spare bedroom. Nick—Pastor Nick—and I, are roommates, if you will. Reluctant roommates. And that's all."

She looked at each member of the council, daring them to say anything to the contrary. For once, it seemed they took her words at face value.

Chris nodded. "I see. So after six months, will you continue living in the parsonage?"

Thankfully, Maura already knew the answer to this question. "No. There's an apartment above the theatre. I plan to renovate it and move in as soon as I'm able."

Her smugness was short-lived. As soon as the words were out of her mouth, she realized she'd never shared this part of the plan with Nick. She glanced over at him, but his face was blank now, devoid of any emotion. She couldn't tell how he felt about this newest bit of information.

"One more question," Chris said. "After the six months is over, how do we know you won't leave town again?"

Maura bit the inside of her lip. She'd really hoped to avoid this question. She didn't know the answer yet, and admitting that wouldn't endear her to the rest of the council. But all she could tell them was the truth.

"You don't know," she said, "because I don't know. If I choose to stay, I'll live in town and run the Music Box. If I choose to leave, I'll sell it and someone else will run it. Either way, Granger benefits."

Chris smiled. "Fair enough," he said with a nod. "Thank you for being so honest and forthright with us. I think your theatre will make a wonderful addition to our community. Oren," he said, turning to the man, "should we vote?"

After all the worry, all the anxiety, and the unexpected grilling from Pastor Chris, it came down to a simple vote of yeas and nays. In less than two minutes time, her plan was approved and the church council sent her on her way, with their blessing.

Maura walked out of the church building and into the courtyard. She'd always found it a beautiful, peaceful place, but today, she appreciated it more than ever. A warm breeze danced through the trees, setting the daisies in a nearby flowerbed to bobbing. It felt so good to be out of that room and standing in the sunshine.

"Ms. Sullivan, wait!"

She turned to see Pastor Chris jogging up to her, his tie flapping off to one side. What was he going to spring on her now?

She crossed her arms. "So you do know I prefer to go by Sullivan?"

He nodded. His cheeks were just slightly pink, either from embarrassment or the exertion of his short run. "Pastor Nick told me, but it wouldn't have helped your case with the others if I'd called you that."

Boy, did he have that one right. But what was he doing out here now? "Shouldn't you have stayed till the end of the meeting?"

Chris dismissed the thought with a wave of his hand. "They don't need me for the rest of the stuff. It's all pretty basic. Besides, I've got a hospital visit to make, which was the perfect excuse to get out of there."

"You're a smart one."

He grew serious. "I also wanted to talk to you before you left. To apologize for asking you all those questions. I know it couldn't have been easy for you."

"Then why did you do it?" Her words came out sharp and bitter, not at all how she'd intended.

"You know how it is with church grapevines. The Bible tells us not to gossip, but it seems most folks think that's just a suggestion. I figured the best way to squash the rumors and the talking was to let you address them straight out. If I crossed a line, I hope you can forgive me."

He was right about the gossip, and he'd found a way to defuse it for her. Apparently, her first impression of him had been right after all. Warmth wrapped around Maura like a blanket on a cold December morning. She wasn't used to having an ally in the church, let alone one of the leadership. She liked this new feeling.

"Now that you've explained, there's nothing to forgive. I appreciate your help in there."

He smiled. "You have more supporters than you might think. Not all of them will come right out and admit it, but I think most of the congregation is rooting for you to succeed. And for you to stay in town."

"And for Nick and me to get back together?" As long as they were speaking freely, she might as well address this.

Chris shrugged. "That would be a natural reaction, don't you think? I can only speak for myself, but I want to see the best possible outcome for both you and Pastor Nick."

A chill struck her as if someone had ripped away the blanket, leaving her exposed to the elements. The man standing in front of her was about her age, but Maura felt as if she could be his mother. His eyes were bright, his expression honest and open. In his world, the Lord worked all things together for good. There was a time when she felt the way he looked. But it seemed like a lifetime ago.

Not trusting herself to speak, she patted his arm and turned, walking out of the parking lot. She couldn't tell him why she and Nick could never truly be husband and wife again. How could she, when she hadn't even told Nick the whole truth?

7

Nick paced the floor of his office, prodding his brain for the right Scripture. This usually wasn't so difficult. He'd always been good at memorization, particularly when it was something important or meaningful. His mother used to tease him, saying his brain was like a water faucet; just turn it on and the facts poured out. But today the faucet sputtered and spit, giving up only a drop or two at a time. Nothing was coming easy.

Nothing except thoughts of Maura.

He went back around the desk and looked down at his sermon notes spread across its top. What a mess. His thoughts hadn't been this jumbled in years. Another image of Maura popped into his head. She was at the council meeting, her dark hair pulled back, sitting rigid in a metal folding chair, taking all the shots that were thrown at her. She'd held her own with the council members, he'd give her that.

Once she started talking about the theatre project, though, her reserve had dropped away and she'd become animated. Nick smiled. It was like the first time she stood in the theatre, and he had watched her transformation from hurt and guarded to open and excited.

Nick's smile twisted downward. It was no wonder he was so confused. Dealing with Maura was like dealing with two different women. One was reserved, keeping her feelings to herself, not wanting to get close to anyone. The other was lively and vibrant, anxious to meet the task at hand. The problem was he never knew which one of them was going to show up.

"Help me, Lord." Nick prayed as he took up his pacing once more. "Help me focus on this sermon."

Husbands, love your wives.

His feet stopped moving. The sermon had nothing to do with spousal relationships. Obviously, he was still distracted with thoughts of Maura.

Nick was on the move again. "Help me focus, Lord."

Husbands, love your wives and do not be bitter toward them.

"Colossians 3:18." Nick sank onto the couch at the other side of the room. Grabbing a Bible, he looked up the verse, just to be sure. Yep, there it was.

Nick stared at the pages of the Bible as it lay across his knees. Was this God trying to tell him something, or his own guilty conscious harping at him? Either way, he couldn't ignore it.

He read the verse again silently. Next he read part of it out loud. "Be not bitter toward them." A hollow place formed in Nick's gut and was quickly filled with burning frustration. Wasn't he entitled to some bitterness? He had loved Maura, but she'd walked out on him.

Why did she leave?

"You tell me." The sarcastic answer came out of Nick so fast it surprised him. He winced, glancing up at the ceiling, waiting for a lightning bolt to slap him upside the head.

Nothing. Just a quiet calm settled on the room, a peacefulness encouraging him to think.

He put the Bible on the table and leaned back on the couch, sinking into the softness of the cushions. He and Maura had been so happy once. Almost from the first moment he saw her, he knew they were meant for each other.

He and a couple of college buddies had gone to Sullivan's because they'd heard the food was good and inexpensive. They got in line, but instead of reading the menu board, Nick couldn't take his eyes off the pretty, dark-haired waitress behind the counter—Maura, according to her nametag.

She looked at the customer ahead of him with a pleasant smile. "How can I help you, sir?"

The tall, thick-waisted man wore a battered ball cap with the name "Bubba" stitched across the back. With his beefy hands splayed on the counter, he slowly looked Maura up and down.

"Well now," he said, "I can think of a few ways you could help me out, but I don't think they're on the menu."

"I'm sorry, sir," she said. "I can only help you with items that are on the menu. May I suggest a corned beef sandwich with a side of coleslaw?"

The man hitched his thumbs in his belt loops, dragging the waistband of his faded jeans dangerously low. "A sandwich sounds mighty fine, but is there something else I can get . . . on the side, that is?"

Maura's cheeks turned red. Nick couldn't take another second of listening to the neanderthal customer and doing nothing. He stepped around Bubba and leaned a hip against the counter. "You might want to try french fries. Or maybe a side of fruit. That's more healthy." He turned his attention to Maura. "Do you have any fruit?"

Her eyes grew wide. "Yes, we have fruit," she answered. Then she looked at Bubba. "Would you like fruit?"

Snickers twittered around every table. Bubba frowned and pulled his wallet from his back pocket. "Yeah, sure. Fruit." He tossed a ten-dollar bill on the counter, and sulked away to a table in the corner.

A relieved Maura Sullivan looked up at Nick Shepherd and said, "Thank you," with so much gratitude that he fell in love with her on the spot. The day they were married was the happiest of his life, and he'd vowed to always protect her and put her needs before his own.

She wanted to see the gopher.

Nick blinked. His call to Granger had come so fast. One of his professors told him about Faith Community, how the congregation wanted someone to assist the ailing senior pastor until another more experienced pastor could take over. The need was immediate, so Nick and Maura spent their honeymoon driving across the country. Maura wanted to enjoy the trip—see some sights—but he'd been consumed by the schedule. His schedule. He'd ignored her needs.

She wanted to spend time with you.

The job took up so much of his time. And just a month after their arrival, Pastor Wesson had a stroke. Suddenly, his temporary mentorship had turned into a request that he take over permanently. Honored to be trusted with such a responsibility, Nick didn't think twice before saying yes.

After that, he was always away at a meeting or involved in some kind of church business. He and Maura hardly saw each other. A chill swept over him like he'd just walked into a meat locker. He'd wanted so badly to please the congregation and not let them down. Instead, he'd let his wife down.

But why did Maura leave? Nick put a hand to his mouth, the thumb pressing into his cheek. He'd neglected her; he saw that now. But why didn't she talk to him instead of leave him?

Be patient.

Nick let out a breath. He could only control his own actions and feelings. He had to let go of any anger he still felt toward

Maura. And he owed her an apology. In time, he hoped she'd tell him what else had driven her to leave. But first things first.

He pushed off the couch and hit his knees. For now, it was time to pray.

———— ✺ ————

Maura pushed through the doors of Rosie's Diner and hurried to the counter.

"Hey, Maura," Josie called out from behind the cash register. "Work through lunch again?" It hadn't taken long for the waitress to get used to Maura's schedule.

"Something like that." She tilted her head, reading the chalkboard behind Josie. "I don't suppose you have any of the lunch special left?"

"You're in luck. Want a Coke with that?"

"Diet." Maura handed over a ten-dollar bill to cover the meal and tip.

"Thanks." Josie put the money in the till with a grin. "I just hope we don't have anymore late lunchers because they'll be out of luck."

Maura laughed. "You mean I'm not the only one?"

Josie jerked a thumb toward the other end of the counter. "Nope. The reverend beat you by a few minutes."

As Josie walked away to fill her order, Maura turned and noticed Nick watching her. She hadn't even seen him.

"Hi, there." She lifted her hand and a slow smile moved over Nick's mouth. Without a word, he motioned to the stool beside him.

"So," she said, sitting down. "You're eating on the run today too?"

He nodded. "I ended up working through lunch."

Old habits died hard. She used to wonder why he did it. How hard could it be to take time to eat a meal? Now that she was in the same position, she understood exactly how it happened.

"Here's your food." Josie held out two brown paper bags. "Let me get your drinks."

As Josie filled to-go cups at the fountain, the tangy smell of cheese steak and onions rose from the bag. Maura's stomach growled. A flush warmed her cheeks as she looked at Nick, whose shoulders shook with silent laughter.

"Guess I'm hungrier than I thought."

"I know the feeling." Nick picked up the cup that Josie set in front of him, nodding his thank you.

After retrieving her drink and grabbing a few extra napkins, Maura headed for the door. Nick held it open for her with his foot.

"Thanks." She scooted around him, careful not to trip on his tasseled loafer.

"No problem. So—" He looked down the street toward the church. Then he looked the other way toward the theatre. "Looks like we're headed in separate directions."

As usual. She nodded.

He lifted his sack and held it swaying between them. "Would you like to eat lunch together?"

His blurted request almost made her drop her soda. "Where?"

He motioned with his head. "We could go over to the park."

Neutral ground. Casual. And preferable to eating alone in her musty, still-dingy office at the theatre. Her stomach growled again. She needed to eat soon, even if that meant digging in right here on the sidewalk.

"Sure. Lead the way."

They walked the block and a half to the park and sat at the first table they came to. Maura pulled her food out of the bag, salivating as she got a fresh whiff of still-hot beef. She started to unroll the sandwich from its paper wrapper but stopped when she noticed Nick hadn't opened his bag yet. He sat across from her, hands in his lap, head bowed. Oops. She put her hands on the edge of the table and waited until after he said "Amen" to attack her food.

Nick ripped the corner from a packet of ketchup and squirted it on his open sandwich wrapper. "I've missed seeing you around the last few days."

Maura looked at him over the luscious Philly cheese steak she'd just bitten into. After they worked out the schedule to avoid embarrassing bathroom mishaps, she and Nick hadn't seen much of each other. She never considered that he might miss her.

"How's it going at the theatre?" he asked.

Now here was a subject she felt comfortable with. She nodded her head as she swallowed. "Good. I hired someone to wash down the walls so I could see what I was dealing with. Now that they're clean, the murals look much better. They just need to be freshened up a bit."

They continued eating and exchanged small talk about Maura's plans. A breeze blew through the park, rustling the leaves of the thick oak trees shimmering above their heads. A bushy tailed squirrel scampered down the trunk of tree near them. Sitting up on its hind legs, it sniffed the air and cocked its head in their direction. Nick tore a piece of bread from his sandwich and threw it to the little beggar who snatched it with his paws, stuffed it in his mouth, and ran back up the tree.

A pang of memory gnawed at Maura's gut. She remembered a similar time when they were still dating. Nick had tossed a french fry to a hungry seagull. As a result they'd been surrounded by a flock of greedy birds, flapping and squawking, demanding more.

It was the day he'd told her about receiving the call to the church in Granger.

"At least the squirrel didn't have any friends."

The sound of Nick's voice pulled her back. She absorbed every detail of his expression—how his eyelids seemed half-closed and his mouth pulled down slightly at one corner. He remembered too. They hadn't known it at the time, but both of their lives had changed that day.

Maura looked down at her half-eaten sandwich. She wasn't hungry anymore.

"We had some good times, didn't we?"

Her head jerked up. "What?"

He pursed his lips and his gaze darted away, then back again. "You and I had a good thing together. But as soon as I accepted the call to pastor here, I started neglecting you." He reached across the table and took her hand. "I'm so sorry for that, Maura."

Her fingers burned where he touched them, the heat radiating through the rest of her body. They had gone for more than six years without any contact. Not a phone call or even a letter. So where had this come from, this sudden concern for her welfare? In spite of her painful memories, a small seed of hope took hold in her heart. Did he finally see her? Was his love for her finally stronger than his responsibility to his flock?

"Why now?" She could barely speak past the lump that had settled in her throat.

His expression turned sheepish. "God made it pretty clear to me what a jerk I've been."

God. The lingering taste of beef and onions turned sour in her mouth. She should be glad he acknowledged his past mistake at all. But the fact that someone else had to tell him, even if it was *God*, felt like sandpaper rubbing against her heart, grinding hope into dust. Couldn't he have figured it out for himself? She yanked her hand from his grasp and started picking up the lunch remains.

"Would you come to church with me this Sunday?"

Her hand stalled in the middle of balling up the sandwich wrapper. "Excuse me?"

"I know these last years have been . . . hard." He rubbed his forehead and frowned. "I can't stand knowing you blame God for my shortcomings. Why don't you come back to church? Take that first step toward rebuilding your faith?"

Pinpricks ignited in Maura's nose and behind her eyes as tears threatened to spill. So that's what this was about—the lunch, the apology. It had nothing to do with her. It was all about Nick's guilty conscience and his constant need to fix whatever was broken.

She stood up slowly. "Let me make this perfectly clear. The last six years of my life have not been good. But it's incredibly arrogant for you to assume that you have anything to do with my relationship with God. I lost you, my father, my home, my business, my—" A single sob choked her, keeping her from blurting out the secret she'd kept hidden all this time. She pulled back her shoulders and swallowed her emotions. "Do us both a favor and concentrate on your flock, Pastor. They need you more than I do."

8

Maura was chasing her tail. Literally.

Not for the first time, she wished for a full-length mirror in the parsonage. Standing at the foot of her bed, she looked behind her, checking out the back of her cargo pants. It was no use. Instead of finding out whether the pocket flaps lay flat, she just went around in a tight circle, making herself dizzy.

This is ridiculous. She put a steadying hand on the nearest wall and stepped into her Keds. It had taken her a good half hour to decide what to wear tonight. Why was she so concerned about how she looked, anyway? She was just going to the Wednesday night youth group meeting. Lainie thought it would be a good idea for Maura to meet the kids before she started to work with them.

"Check them out in their natural habitat," the genial youth leader had joked.

And if anyone knew about being checked out, it was Maura. During the weeks following the council meeting, she'd been like a specimen under a microscope. She had meetings and consultations with everyone from carpenters to plumbers to pavers, and it seemed her reputation preceded her with all of them. If they weren't members of Nick's church, they at least knew about the situation with Miss Hattie's will. Her first exchanges with new people were always interesting.

"Well, nice to finally meet the infamous Mrs. Shepherd."

"How are you liking life in Granger this time around?"

But one had become her personal favorite, "So *you're* the one who ran off on Pastor Nick!"

Each time, Maura had gone through the same basic speech. "Nice to meet you. I go by Ms. Sullivan now. Since this is a business meeting, I'd prefer not to talk about my personal life, but I can assure you I'm happy to be in Granger."

It got to the point where Maura considered having cards printed up so she could hand them to people upon first contact and avoid rattling off what had now become a well-rehearsed monologue.

Despite the discomfort that usually prefaced her business meetings, they had gone well. She'd been surprised at the skilled labor available to her in the small town. A Granger native, Rachel had proved an invaluable resource when it came to finding the right person for the job.

If only things were as smooth on the home front. Ever since their impromptu lunch in the park, the tenuous relationship between her and Nick had been strained. Thankfully, they both had such full schedules that they rarely crossed paths. But occasionally they'd bump into each other at the house, and a storm cloud settled in the room. It was a difficult living arrangement to begin with, but her refusal to attend Sunday services made it worse.

Which made it all the more ironic that she now stood in her room, preparing to attend a youth group meeting at the church. It was the last place she thought she'd end up.

"Oh, just get over it," she muttered, snatching her purse from a chair in the corner. "You're a grown woman. Start acting like it."

With a determined nod, she flicked the light switch and left the room. At the same time, the front door flew open and Nick and Lainie stumbled into the house. Nick's deep, throaty rumble mixed with Lainie's bubbly giggle. It took her by surprise. Nick sounded happy.

Maura took a moment to soak in the scene. She hadn't seen Nick truly enjoy himself in quite some time. Certainly, there hadn't been a lot to laugh about since her return to this house. Even before that, during the last months they'd lived together as husband and wife, their interaction had been strained. Frustration seemed to be the emotion they most often had in common.

Looking at him now brought back warm memories of the young man who first captured her heart. She'd almost forgotten how his face opened up when he laughed, as if he laid his soul bare for all to see. She didn't want to admit, but it hurt that another woman could get such a response from him.

They hadn't noticed her yet, and she knew that the longer she kept her mouth shut, the more uncomfortable it would be when they realized she'd been hiding in the shadows. She strode down the hall. "So what's the joke?"

Her voice came out all wrong, loud and sharp, Nick and Lainie obviously took it the way it sounded. They both froze, looking down the dimly lit hallway to where Maura stood. Nick quickly reverted to his irritated, closed off self. And Lainie, well, if Maura didn't know better, she'd say that Lainie looked guilty. Which was just plain silly. Lainie didn't have anything to be guilty about, did she?

Maura made herself smile and walk toward them. "Sounds like you two were having a good time. That's . . . good."

Terrific, she'd gone from sounding harsh to sounding brainless. This just wasn't working. Better to say nothing at all.

So she didn't, and the three of them stood there, looking at one another.

"I came to get you for the meeting, but I ran into Pastor Nick outside," Lainie piped up.

Nick added, "I just finished blessing a cow."

Maura blinked. "A cow?"

"A calf, actually. One of our members is very serious about 1 Corinthians 10:31."

Maura had no clue when it came to matching scriptures to their verses. She could barely manage to remember all the words in the right order. But Nick had a real knack for it.

"Which is?"

"So whether you eat or drink, or whatever you do, do it all for the glory of God," Nick said in his best pastor's voice. "Whenever this man gets new livestock, he wants me to bless it."

It was wild, even for Granger. "How could you possibly have time to go bless every new animal that shows up on a farm?" Her mind raced. "It's not so bad if he just has cows. But what about chickens? Do you have to run out there every time one lays an egg?"

"That's what we were laughing about," Lainie yelped. "Pastor told me about the calf blessing, and I said, can you imagine if he had chickens?"

Maura and Lainie started laughing, drawing a slow smile out of Nick. "Thankfully," he said with a shrug, "the main thrust of the operation is corn, so there aren't many animals on his farm. And no chickens."

"So who is this pious farmer?" Maura asked once she'd stopped laughing.

"I can't tell you that."

Maura looked at Lainie, but the young woman just shook her head. "I can't help you. He wouldn't tell me, either."

"It's for your own good, trust me. You know how people talk. I wouldn't want either of you drawn into any gossip about him at church." His smile slipped, and he looked pointedly at Maura. "Not that there's any great danger of that."

The unexpected dig made Maura wince. She had no comeback.

"Don't be so quick to judge, Pastor. The whole reason I'm here is to pick up Maura for our Wednesday night youth group meeting." The humor had left Lainie's voice, and it took on a serious tone. She chuckled, as if to soften the rebuke. "Who knows, we could cross paths with your mystery farmer."

"Highly unlikely. The man I'm talking about doesn't attend church. He's something of a hermit. But he's a hermit with strong faith." Nick nodded at each of them. "You two have a nice time. If you'll excuse me, I've got some work to do."

He walked past Maura, hugging the wall to avoid brushing against her on the way to his office. The sharp sound of the door closing cut into the empty silence of the house.

Poor Lainie. One look at her and Maura could tell she wanted to say something, but what was there to say? Best to pretend this never happened.

"Let's go," Maura said, motioning toward the front door. "I'm anxious to meet your kids."

———— ✺ ————

Lainie moved to the middle of the room and held up her hands. "Pipe down, guys! Time to get started!"

For a little person, she had a powerful voice. The kids didn't stop talking at once, but Lainie raised her arms, rotating like the lens in a lighthouse until she had absolute quiet.

"Thanks," she said with a smile. "I'll open us up in prayer, unless somebody else wants to."

There were no takers. As Lainie said a quick prayer, thanking God for bringing them together and for what He was about to do, Maura snuck a closer look at the kids.

When Lainie invited her to come, she'd had a picture in her head of what the youth group meeting would be like. She'd imagined clean-cut kids sitting in chairs arranged in a neat circle, heads bent over their Bibles, raising their hands to participate in the discussion and afterward, sharing punch and cookies as a treat. It was a scene straight from an old black and white movie. Thankfully, this group shattered her preconceptions.

Teenage bodies, some sitting on the floor, some in bean bag chairs, and some on huge pillows, filled the room. Most of them wore casual clothes, although a few looked trendy. Cans of soda and bags of chips and cheese puffs littered the floor. As soon as Lainie finished her prayer the noise level rose again. It ebbed and peaked, depending on the excitement of the speaker. It reminded Maura of her own youth group when she was a teen.

Lainie held up her hands again, regaining control of the room. "You've probably noticed our guest." Lainie walked over to Maura and pulled her to her feet. "This is Maura Sullivan. She's renovating the Music Box, and we're going to give her a hand."

A chorus of moans rose from the group, setting off a matching response inside Maura. This was not good. Her helpers were already disgruntled, and they didn't even know what she wanted yet.

"It's not as bad as it sounds." Maura added some bounce to her voice, hoping her enthusiasm would be contagious. "With all of you pitching in, it might even be fun. And when it's all done, I hope some of you will get involved in the actual theatre . . . you know, plays, concerts, acting classes, that kind of thing."

Acting classes? Now why had she said that? Maura hadn't even considered acting classes as part of her master plan, but suddenly, it made perfect sense. And it seemed to strike a chord with some of the young people. A few of them visibly brightened, nudging the person next to them.

"See," Lainie said as she jumped in, "this is a situation where you sow some hard work and you reap a whole lot of fun."

"Aren't you married to Pastor Nick?"

The question came from the back of the room and made both Maura and Lainie whip their heads around in surprise.

"Who wants to know?" Lainie asked.

A boy at the back of the room shot up his hand and put it down just as quickly. "If you and Pastor Nick are married, how come you aren't Maura Shepherd?"

Lainie turned to Maura, sympathy clear on her face. "Do you want to answer that?"

Truthfully, no, she didn't. But Maura knew if she ignored the question, she'd give the teens something to talk about— something to speculate over and make a bigger deal out of it than it was. So even though she'd like nothing better than to walk out of the room, Maura smiled, taking a moment to gather her thoughts before she answered.

"Pastor Nick and I had some problems and we split up several years ago. It doesn't seem right to use his name when we're not a couple anymore."

"But you didn't get divorced?" This came from a girl sitting up toward the front. By the intensity on her face, Maura guessed the girl had personal experience with the subject.

"No, we didn't. And I'm not going to get into the details. But I can tell you that the reason I'm back here now is because Miss Hattie Granger left the theatre to me. And that's why I live in the parsonage with Pastor Nick. It was one of the conditions of her will."

That seemed to satisfy most of them.

"So Maura changed her last name because of what it symbolizes." Lainie jumped in, once again coming to Maura's rescue. "That goes right along with what I wanted to talk about tonight. We need to pick a name for our group."

Using examples from the Bible and from history, Lainie explained how names have meanings and how important they are. Maura found the discussion interesting and tried to stay focused, but her mind wouldn't cooperate.

Why hadn't she divorced Nick? Their relationship was broken to the point that she felt compelled to leave. Divorce would be the next logical step. While she'd certainly thought about it, it was never something she had the stomach to follow up on. And what about Nick? According to Rachel, he'd been presented with the opportunity to pursue a divorce, absolved from consequences by the church council. Yet he hadn't taken it. Now they were back together, a married couple living as virtual strangers. No wonder they were both having such a hard time moving forward.

Heaviness settled in Maura's chest. They couldn't go on this way. If she stayed in Granger, she and Nick had two choices: either permanently sever their marital ties with a divorce, or . . . There was another option, but it was so out of the realm of possibility, she hated to even think about it. Though Maura had no reason to believe it could happen, the mere thought lifted her sadness, and for a moment, she let herself bask in the possibility.

Reconciliation.

9

There's a pretty good-sized crowd out there." Pastor Chris entered Nick's office. "I guess you were right about adding a second service."

Nick smiled as he adjusted his tie. "Sometimes, I manage to get it right. Of course, it's usually when I'm repeating what the Lord's already told me."

Strains of music filtered through the door as the praise band started the first song. Nick pulled the door open, feeling the rush of the music as it grew louder. "Time to get out there."

Chris nodded, stepping ahead of him but stopping in the doorway. "Say, it's great that Maura's here today."

Nick blinked. "What? You saw Maura? Here?"

"Yeah, I saw her walk in with Lainie." Chris crossed his arms and cocked his head at Nick. "You mean you didn't know she was here?"

"That woman is full of surprises." *At least this is a good one.* His attempt to apologize for past mistakes and to draw her back to the church had been a miserable failure. They'd hardly spoken since that disastrous lunch in the park. He had no idea what brought her here today.

But now, he had more important work to do. He couldn't let himself be distracted by the shambles of his personal life. It was time to focus on the Lord and ministering to His people. Nick took a deep breath. *No matter what I say or do, let them hear and see you, Lord.*

———∞∞∞———

Maura stood in the back of the sanctuary, wondering again how she'd let Lainie talk her into this. She'd been attending the youth group meetings for the last three weeks and even looked forward to them. But then Lainie had come up with the idea of having Maura help during the Sunday service.

"It would be so great," she'd said while bouncing on the balls of her feet and sending her ponytail swinging. "I'm always looking for new ways to get the point across, and drama is perfect. You could lead the kids through some skits."

Maura resisted at first, but Lainie persisted. "Look at it this way, if you're going to teach drama classes at your theatre, what better way to get the kids interested? Give them a little taste of it now."

She had a point. Besides, if Maura worked with the kids, she wouldn't have to talk to the rest of the congregation. She could just slip in and slip out. That way, she could avoid actually attending the service.

Lainie had neglected to tell her that the youth group stayed in the church for the beginning of the service and worshiped with the congregation before leaving for their own study time.

From her spot by the wall, Maura watched the sanctuary fill up. Wanting to snag a seat in the back before they were gone, Maura slipped into a pew, trying not to attract any attention. She looked down at her lap, pretending to read the bulletin in her hands, only to avoid making eye contact with anyone. Her eyes grew wide when she saw the monthly church calendar printed on the back. Almost every day had some event, meeting, or class inked in. And Nick probably attended every one of them.

Maura looked up at the front of the church. As clearly as if it was happening at that very moment, she remembered the day Nick was installed as senior pastor. He knelt before the altar, surrounded by the church elders. They reached out, their hands touching his shoulders, back, head, wherever they could find a spot. They prayed to impart a blessing, but to Maura, it meant something else. From the moment she and Nick arrived in Granger, someone was always reaching out for him, grabbing him, needing his time, his prayer, his attention. As the prayers continued up front, the people sitting in the pews around Maura reached out, laying their hands on her. And in that moment, she knew they wouldn't stop at Nick. As the pastor's wife, they were already reaching out for her too.

A hand fell on her shoulder. Maura jumped and her shoulders tightened as she turned to see who stood behind her. She whooshed out a sigh of relief as Rachel slid into the pew beside her.

"I had to look twice to make sure it was you." Rachel took her hand and squeezed it. "It's so good to see you here."

"Thanks. Where are Derrick and the kids?"

"They're sitting up there." She wiggled her finger toward the front of the church.

Maura shifted in her seat, not liking the idea of splitting up a family. "Wouldn't you rather sit with them?"

"No, I sit with them every Sunday. It's been too long since I had the chance to worship with you."

Maura didn't know what to say. In some weird way, it felt good to be back in a church with a friend sitting next to her.

Kind of like putting on a pair of unstylish, but remarkably comfortable shoes. She didn't want to like it, but part of her did. Thankfully, the band began to play, so she didn't have to think about it. The congregation rose to its feet to sing a lively song of praise. It was one Maura hadn't heard before, but she followed along as best she could.

After another upbeat number, the music slowed, becoming sweet and contemplative. This one, Maura knew. The song asked God for more of His love, more of His power. She recognized it as one of Nick's favorites. Up until that point, Maura had resisted the urge to look for him, but now she couldn't stop herself. With just a small turn of her head, she zeroed in on him. He left his spot in the front pew and moved up the platform steps, stopping in front of the altar. Singing all the while, he joined the worship team as they led the congregation. His eyes closed, and he raised his hands slightly, as if he was open and ready to receive whatever God had in store for him.

An electric jolt surged through Maura. She experienced more than mere awareness of Nick—more than her attraction to him as a man. Somehow, she felt the connection he had with the Lord. There had been a time in her life when she could lose herself in worship and feel that it was just her and God, communicating on a personal, intimate level, even when other people surrounded her. She could tell Nick was in that place now, and for a moment, she yearned to feel it too.

Rachel casually tucked a tissue into Maura's hand. Embarrassed, Maura dabbed at her eyes just as the tears started to fall, hoping the mascara she'd put on that morning hadn't run all over her face.

How could she let this happen? She should know by now that it was all part of the big show. The emotion, the music, it all played on you, made you open up, so God could come in and knock you over. WHAM! Your husband belongs to me.

Wham! Your life is not your own. Wham! I've taken away everyone who ever mattered to you.

No, she'd been on the receiving end of God's love once, and she wasn't about to let her defenses down again.

Maura grabbed the edges of her ragged emotions and pulled them tightly around her as the song faded to a close. By the time the praise team moved away from the microphones and down to the pews, Maura was back in control. Standing front and center, Nick welcomed the congregation and released the youth group to go to its study. With a flutter-fingered good-bye to Rachel, Maura popped from her seat, more than ready to follow Lainie and the teenagers out of the sanctuary.

"Today, I thought we'd talk about weeds."

The teenagers stared at Lainie in confusion. One stocky boy, who looked like he was built to be a linebacker, dug his elbow into the ribs of the fellow next to him.

"The sheriff already stopped by the high school and gave us that talk. We know we're supposed to run from weed."

"Crack is whack!" his buddy yelled out.

Laughter filled the room, and several of the kids shot their arms into the air, hands balled into fists, and shouted together "Just say no!"

Sitting in the back of the room, Maura covered her mouth with one hand, holding back a full-blown belly laugh. Lainie didn't hold anything back, making a show of rolling her eyes and laughing along with the teenagers. "Sheriff Reynolds will be thrilled to find out he made such an impact on you. But I'm not talking about *weed*. I'm talking about *weeds*. The kind you find in your garden."

A chorus of moans filled the room, heads sagged, and shoulders crumpled. Maura had been skeptical when Lainie had first approached her with the idea of using weeds to illustrate this lesson. After all, how many teenagers knew anything about gardening? But Lainie was confident it would work. Judging from the reaction in the room, not only were these kids familiar with the subject of weeds, they had strong opinions about them.

"I see you know the kind I'm talking about," Lainie went on. "The ones you just can't kill, no matter how many times your mom or dad sends you out to deal with them. Well, that's what unforgiveness is like. It sits in your heart, plants its big, stubborn roots, and it grows up into this ugly, life-sucking monster."

She made come-to-me motions with her hands, calling Danielle and Steven, two of the more outgoing members of the group, to the front. "Danni is mad at Steven."

"I am?" The girl glanced over at her friend and gave him a wink.

Lainie nodded. "Yes, for this dramatic illustration, you are." She turned back to the group. "Let's say he . . . he promised to help Danni study for a test, but he went to a party instead, and she ended up flunking."

Danni shook her head. "Not cool, Ace."

Steven shrugged his shoulders as a cocky grin spread across his face. "Sorry, dude. Something came up."

"Steven's sorry," Lainie said, pointing at the boy. "But Danni doesn't care. She's just not going to forgive him. And that's when things start to get messy."

Maura heard her cue. From her spot in the back, she slunk forward, making her way to the front of the room.

Lainie crooked a thumb at her. "Enter Unforgiveness."

Maura latched on to Danni, putting a hand on each of the girl's shoulders and pulling at her just a bit.

Lainie turned back to the other kids in the room. "Whatever Danni does now, she's dragging Unforgiveness along with her." She strolled over to Danni, pretending to run into her on the street. "Hi, Danni. How're you doing today?"

Maura pulled down on Danni's shoulders, making the ugliest face she could behind the girl's back. Giggles erupted throughout the room.

"Not too good," Danni answered, wobbling a little as Maura exerted more pressure. "To tell you the truth, I feel weighed down."

Lainie nodded. "Maybe it's because you're still mad at Steven. You know, he told me he feels pretty bad about what happened. Maybe you should forgive him."

From behind her, Maura now slipped her arms around the front of Danni's neck, pretending to choke the girl. With her head looking over Danni's shoulder, she said in a stage whisper, "How do you know he won't do it again?"

Playing along, Danni choked out the words, "I don't."

Lainie signaled with her hand, cuing Steven, who ran up to Danni. "Danni, I'm really, really sorry about not helping you with the test. Can you please forgive me?"

Danni looked over at the other members of the youth group. "I think I'd better before this unforgiveness kills me." She turned her head back toward Steven. "Yes, I forgive you."

Steven moved forward to hug Danni, and as he did, he pulled Maura's hands from around the girl's neck and pushed her backward. As the two teens hugged, Maura made a big show of falling to the ground, moaning and groaning, effectively dying.

The group applauded as Danni and Steven went back to their seats, and Maura, staying in character, crawled to the back of the room.

Clapping, Lainie moved to the middle of the room. "As you just saw, unforgiveness will suck all the joy out of you if you let it."

Lainie continued to speak to the group, but Maura's mind branched off in a myriad of different directions.

Brushing off the knees of her dress pants, she decided a change was in order. If she was going to make a habit of crawling around on the floor, she should probably start wearing jeans to youth group meetings.

She looked up, spotting Danni and Steven. They were naturals when it came to improvisation. She'd have to talk to them about joining her acting classes once she got them started.

When she could think of no other distractions, Maura examined her own heart. She had tried so hard for so long to put Nick out of her mind and ignore any lingering feelings she had toward him. But today, as she played the weed of unforgiveness, all those emotions had been stirred up. The heaviness, the ugliness, all of it came from a place inside her that was still mad at Nick for pushing her to the point where she felt she had no choice but to leave him. And when she whispered in Danni's ear and asked, "How do you know he won't do it again?" the question had come straight from her own heart.

It was time to face it; she was still angry with Nick. And she didn't trust him. She was afraid that if she forgave him and let her guard down he would hurt her again.

"See you Wednesday!"

Lainie's call to the departing teenagers brought Maura out of her reverie. The class was over, and the room emptied in less than a minute.

"I'm always amazed at the mess teenagers leave behind," Lainie said good-naturedly as she stacked chairs. "I didn't even see anybody eating today, and there are still crumbs all over the floor. Oh, well, they all seemed to have a good time. And mixing it up with that little drama was a big hit. Thanks for rolling with it."

"That's what I'm here for," Maura answered. "It was fun. I think we can do a lot more with the group."

Maura picked up the last chair and moved it off to the side of the room. Though she tried to concentrate on cleaning, thoughts of Nick nagged at her. She needed to forgive him, if for no other reason than to get this weight off her chest. But it wouldn't be as easy as it had been for Danni and Steven in their little skit.

"You know," she said to Lainie, who was pushing a carpet sweeper across the floor, "the whole topic of unforgiveness is interesting. It got me to thinking . . . what if you need to forgive someone for something they don't know they did? In order to forgive them, you'd have to tell them how they hurt you. In that case, wouldn't forgiving them be more painful than just keeping it to yourself?"

Maura hoped her question came off as casual musing. But when Lainie turned to her, she could see the youth leader knew it was more personal than hypothetical. Thankfully, Lainie didn't dig for more details.

"Actually, the most important part of forgiving someone goes on in your heart. If someone hurt you, and you truly forgive that person in your heart, it will show in your actions toward him or her in the future. And sometimes, we need to forgive someone who's not around to talk back. The key is letting go of your anger and hurt and extending forgiveness from your heart, even if it's not face-to-face. After that, you just need to stand back and let God do the rest."

Why did God always have to wind up in the middle of everything? She'd certainly never forgiven Him for the events of the past few years. This would be harder than she'd thought.

Well, one step at a time. She needed to forgive Nick. That much was certain. After today, she felt she was ready to do it.

The church campus appeared empty by the time Maura and Lainie left the youth room. There were still a few cars in the parking lot, but not another person could be seen.

"The place sure clears out fast after service," Maura said.

Lainie nodded. "Unless it's our monthly coffee fellowship hour, people usually scoot out of here pretty quick. Lunch time, you know. And speaking of lunch, would you like to get a bite? I'm starving."

Maura was hungry. But more than that, she thought how nice it would be to have lunch with someone and not just take a sandwich back to the empty theatre where she spent most of her time. "Yeah, that'd be great."

As they went to Lainie's car, the outer door to the church office opened. Pastors Chris and Nick walked out, both looking a little drained after a full morning.

"Hey, you two," Lainie waved. "You finally getting out of here?"

Chris nodded. "We're on our way to lunch."

Maura looked at Nick. Their eyes caught and held. This was it. She needed to do it now. *I forgive you, Nick.* The thought rushed through her, and Maura felt as though something actually snapped in her head. She smiled and without thinking, she asked, "Would the two of you like to join us?"

There it was—her olive branch to Nick. It didn't completely demolish all that stood between them, but at least she'd started to chip away at it. For his part, Nick looked completely shocked at her invitation. Then the corners of his mouth turned up ever so slightly. In a soft voice he answered, "That would be nice."

10

Sitting in his home office, Nick shut the Bible in his lap, bent his head, and said a quick prayer. Preparation for this morning's men's breakfast had gone well, and his spirits were particularly high.

He always looked forward to the third Saturday of the month when the men's study group got together. It was a time when they could share what was going on in their lives and bond over hotcakes and sausage links. But that wasn't the only reason for his positive mood.

An image of Maura barged into his head, bringing a smile to his lips. Co-existing with her had certainly been different since she showed up at church last week. She hadn't come right out and told him, but he could tell that her feelings toward him had changed. Softened a little. They were both so busy they rarely occupied the house at the same time, but when they did bump into each other, the strain was gone. No longer did she scrutinize his every move, waiting for him to make a mistake or say something wrong. It was like the wall she'd erected between them when she came back to Granger had dropped a bit. He could see over it now without standing on his tiptoes.

It seemed the two of them had actually become friends again. And that was a really nice feeling.

Nick pushed himself out of his chair and left his office, nearly colliding with Maura, as she marched down the hall, cell phone pressed to her ear.

"No." She jumped out of Nick's way, waving her free hand at him. She started pacing around the living room. "No, that won't work . . . I understand that, but there's got to be a way . . . I see . . . Then that's what we'll do. I'll find a way to get those seats over to you by the end of the day."

Seats? Nick tugged at his earlobe. Now what was Maura into?

She snapped her cell phone shut, turning to him as she did so. "Was I too loud? Did I disturb you?"

Nick dismissed her concern with a shake of his head. "No, I was just on my way out. Men's breakfast today. What's all this about seats?"

Maura let out a big puff of air, making her bangs do the wave across her forehead. "The theatre seats need to be reupholstered. You know what condition they're in. I had the details all worked out with this fellow in Beaver Falls, but now his truck's broken down, so he can't come get the hardware to recover it, and to top it all off, his daughter just called to tell him she's getting married in November, so if he doesn't start on my job right away, there's no way it'll get done in time for the grand opening, which means I've got to find a way to remove all those seats today and get them to Beaver tonight."

Nick had no idea how she'd said all that in one breath, but he'd managed to follow along. "So what are you going to do?"

"I'm going to the theatre and I'm going to start ripping out seats," she answered, determination clear on her face. "I'll call Rachel on the way and see if she can find a truck to rent." She grabbed her purse and headed for the front door.

"Have you had any breakfast?" Nick called after her.

She turned around, backing toward the door as she answered. "I keep a stash at the theatre. Bottled water and protein bars. I'll just grab a couple of those."

With a wave, she was out the door and on her way. Nick shook his head. He hadn't seen this side of Maura when they'd lived together as a married couple. When they moved to Granger, he'd tried so hard to get her involved in things at the church, but the more he encouraged her, the more she withdrew, until one day, she was completely gone.

But now she'd thrown herself into this theatre project with abandon. And he could only hope her visit to church hadn't been a one-time occurrence. Lainie told him afterward what a great job Maura did working with the kids, using drama to illustrate biblical principles.

It was as if God reached down and slapped the back of Nick's head at that moment. He finally got it. All the activities he'd pushed Maura to do in the past—the ladies' Bible study, potlucks, hospital visitation ministry—none of them were part of Maura's gifting. If he'd stepped back and let her take her time, given her the opportunity to discover what she was passionate about, their lives might be different now.

Just that morning, he'd read in Romans that, though everyone is part of the body of Christ, each person has different gifts and serves different functions. Nick had planned on sharing that nugget with the men's group at breakfast, but now it took on a much larger meaning.

Grabbing his car keys and cell phone, Nick jogged out of the house.

JENNIFER ALLEE

Maura stood in front of the stage, looking out at the rows and rows of bedraggled seats that filled the theatre. The task overwhelmed her, and for a moment, she gave herself over to the feeling. How would she ever accomplish this? She didn't even know if she had the right tools.

Stop it. She wasn't alone. Rachel knew somebody who knew somebody who owned a semi, and she was sure they could hire him and his rig for the day. That was one problem down. All she had to do now was start removing bolts and get the stuff ready to go.

But she was only one woman. How could she possibly do all of this by herself?

I can do all things through Christ, who strengthens me.

Maura frowned. Random Scriptures rarely popped into her head. It must be from all the time she'd spent with Lainie. And while she liked the thought of gaining strength from someone greater than herself, what Maura most needed was physical help. Another dozen or so pairs of hands could help her out of this mess.

Ask, and it shall be given to you.

This time, the Scripture that intruded on her thoughts brought Maura up short. What was going on here? It was like a challenge from God.

A challenge to trust Him.

"Okay, I'm probably an idiot, but I'm desperate." Her voice echoed through the cavernous space. "So I'm asking. If you care about me so much, send me some help." She paused and then added, "Please."

She stood absolutely still, waiting for the doors to burst open, or for muscular, tool-wielding men to drop from the ceiling. She counted the seconds until she got to ten. Eleven. Twelve.

Nothing.

A wave of sadness washed over Maura, pushing her shoulders down into a beaten slump. What had she expected? She'd been a fool to get her hopes up.

There was work to be done, and she'd have to do it herself. Maura knelt down to get a good look at the bolts anchoring the seats to the floor.

With a mighty groan, the lobby door opened. At the sound, Maura jerked upright, her heart thumping in her chest.

In walked Rachel and her kids, wearing grubby clothes, armed with wrenches and other tools, ready to work. Maura blew out a slow breath. Just as she'd thought; her phone call to Rachel had produced more assistance than her begging to God.

"Hey!" Rachel called from the back of the theatre. "We're all set. The truck will be here in about an hour. We'll have no trouble getting this place emptied out."

Maura put one hand on her hip and waved a wrench with the other. "Your positive attitude is refreshing. But in case you hadn't noticed, there are about two-hundred seats in here and only four of us."

"I'm fully aware of how big the job is," Rachel answered, sounding smug. "But your body count is off. I ran into more helpers out in the parking lot."

The doors to the lobby opened again, and the auditorium filled with the noise of at least a dozen men led by Nick. They fanned out through the room, inspecting the seats and discussing what tools would be needed for the job.

Nick walked up to Maura, giving her a brief salute. "Reporting for duty, Ma'am."

"But what about your breakfast?"

"We brought it with us. There are donuts and coffee in the lobby for anybody who wants them."

Every muscle in Maura's body tightened, from her throat to her chest and all the way down to her toes. "I don't understand."

"God reminded me it's more important to live out what the Bible says than to just talk about it. So instead of gathering at a restaurant, here we are." Nick smiled at her, but all Maura could see was the love of God.

You see, I do care.

The thought filled her, and Maura let go of the control she'd held onto for so long. For the first time in years, she believed she wasn't alone.

"Thank you," she whispered and stepped toward Nick, arms open. He hesitated for a moment, but he reached out, pulling her into his embrace. He smoothed her hair with one hand and whispered back, "You're welcome."

The day took off in a flurry of nonstop activity. Not long after the arrival of Nick and his crew, Lainie showed up with half the youth group. The physical act of unbolting the seats from the floor turned out to be even more difficult than it looked, so that task was delegated to the men. Meanwhile, Rachel and Lainie supervised the teens in wiping the dust and cobwebs from the old seats and loading them in the truck. Maura went from seat to seat, using masking tape to mark the ones that were beyond salvaging and needed to be tossed into the dumpster. When that was done, she pitched in wherever she could.

At lunch time, someone ordered pizza, and the whole group took a break. Sitting in the lobby, surrounded by men and teenagers, Maura realized this was a part of the congregation she hadn't interacted with when she and Nick first moved to

Granger. She'd been so preoccupied with the church council members, the casserole-bearing Ladies' Auxiliary, and all the other groups she felt uncomfortable in, she hadn't considered there were others she might click with. She and Rachel were close friends, largely because Rachel made a point to get to know her without asking her to be the head of anything. But Rachel was the exception.

She'd felt so alone during that time. But now she was surrounded with people who not only cared about her, but who gave up their Saturday to help her out of a bind. It was pretty amazing.

She also took the time to really see Nick. Sitting cross-legged on the floor and holding a paper plate full of pizza, he talked and laughed with the men near him. A few of the boys had joined the group, and he made a point to include them in the conversation. She'd seen him like this before. No matter what group he was in, Nick could always find something to talk about. People were drawn to him because when he asked, "How are you doing?" he sincerely wanted to know the answer.

She finally acknowledged that this was the real Nick. He'd never tried to hide it from her. Since the day she'd first met him, she knew how much he cared about the people around him. She'd even found it endearing, until it took his time away from her. When that happened, she'd fought it till she was worn out and beaten.

Maura would never be like Nick. She couldn't go into a room and instantly feel comfortable with everybody in it. But she finally began to understand that was okay. During the past few weeks, she'd discovered that when she followed her heart, getting involved in projects that inspired her, she acted more like Nick than she ever thought possible. Now it was a little easier for her to understand why he got so caught up in his work.

Lainie stood up from her spot on the floor and started collecting empty pizza boxes. "Okay, everybody, it's time to get back to work!"

A chorus of good-natured groans followed as teens and adults started picking up their lunch trash. Within a few minutes, the pizza party was over, and Maura's volunteer crew was back to work.

Maura stopped Lainie at the lobby door. "You're a real slave driver, you know that?"

Lainie gave her a mock salute. "Yes, Ma'am, I do."

"Why do you think I hired her?" Nick tossed a soda can in the trash and approached them.

"That's right. In my interview Pastor Nick asked me if I had any qualms about whipping kids into shape. I told him no-sir-ee. In fact, that's what I do for fun."

Nick and Lainie laughed. Jealousy whispered in Maura's ear, and she turned away, wondering just how close the two of them were.

Something across the room caught Lainie's attention. "Excuse me. I need to wrangle up a couple of my kids."

As she took off, Nick put his hand on Maura's shoulder. He bent down slightly, looking straight into her eyes. "Lainie has never been anything to me but a friend and colleague."

Maura looked around frantically to make sure no one was close enough to overhear them. "How did you know I even . . . I mean . . . I never said . . ."

Nick put a finger to her lips. "You didn't have to."

She pulled his hand away from her face, but didn't let him go. "That's good to know."

Maura had never wanted to kiss him more than she did at that moment. But the spell was broken when someone called out, "Maura! I found an old ring on the floor. Can I keep it?"

"Sorry. I need to take care of that." Her voice sounded husky and deep.

Nick smiled and let go of her hand. "That's okay. I know where to find you."

———

By six o'clock that night the fully loaded truck was on its way to Beaver Falls. Inside the theatre Maura thanked everyone and received several good-bye hugs before they left. Nick, being Nick, walked out to the parking lot to see them off personally.

Maura sat on the lip of the stage, her legs dangling over the side, surveying the empty space. Now that the seats were gone, she could see how dirty the floor was. It needed to be cleaned before the refinishers came. The carpeting that ran up the aisles was beyond saving; it needed to be torn up and replaced. And, of course, there were the walls, which also would have to be touched up before anything was done to the floor. Maura pushed the to-do list from her mind. She and Rachel had made a timeline for all of the work to be done. Thanks to the help they'd received today, they were still right on schedule.

The lobby door hinges squealed, and Nick walked back in, his steps echoing down the side aisle as he approached her.

"Everybody's on their way home," he said. He skirted the orchestra pit and climbed up the stage steps. He dropped next to Maura and followed her gaze. "Wow. It looks bigger now."

She nodded. "Spaces always look bigger when they're empty."

"Funny," he said after a moment, "our house felt smaller after you'd gone."

A few weeks ago, that comment would have infuriated her. But now, she saw the sad truth in his words.

"Why do you think she did it?"

Nick turned to her. "Who did what?"

"Miss Hattie. Why do you think she gave me this place?"

"I don't know. She never talked to me about it. Did you ever tell her about your dream of owning a theatre?"

Maura thought back. "No. But once I ran into her in the grocery store, and she started talking to me about destiny."

"In the grocery store?"

"Right in the middle of the produce section. She told me that even though I was called to be your wife, God had a higher calling for me—something only I could do—and that I needed to find out what that was."

Nick let out a low whistle. "She got that right. I guess God filled in the blanks for her."

Maura nodded. "I guess so."

They sat in silence for a while. Maura waited for it to feel awkward, but it didn't. It felt like the most natural thing in the world to sit with him, and when he put his arm around her, she rested her head against his shoulder without a second thought.

"What are we doing, Maura?" Nick asked, his voice soft.

She hadn't thought it through, but their relationship had changed again today. Another piece of the wall had been knocked over. "I'm not sure. I think we're getting to know each other again."

She felt Nick nod against the top of her head. "This may sound crazy, but it kind of feels like we're dating."

Maura laughed and sat back, looking at him. "That's funny, especially since we're living together."

"Well, we are married."

"Yes, there's that."

Nick took her hand. "Maura, there's nothing I'd like better right now than to take you out for a nice dinner. But I can't."

Maura frowned. "Why not?"

"Because you're filthy."

She yanked her hand from his and gave him a playful punch in the shoulder. "Look in a mirror, buddy. You're kind of a mess yourself."

"I'm sure I am." Nick stood up, dusting off the front of his jeans. "How about we go home, get cleaned up, and dig some leftovers out of the fridge?"

He offered her his hand and pulled her to her feet. She was inches away from him. If she took another step closer, she'd be back in his arms. Her heart urged her forward, but her head told her otherwise.

"Leftovers at home," she said, taking a step back. "Right now, that sounds perfect."

11

Are you sure these figures are right?"

Looking at the charts and papers littering Rachel's kitchen table, Maura held her excitement in check. So much had been going right lately, she hesitated to believe that the streak would continue and they would finish the renovation on schedule.

"Absolutely." Rachel looked over her shoulder from where she stood at the counter by the stove. "Do you want me to go over it with you again?"

Through the small window over the sink Maura could see the first snow of the season wafting down, making the bare tree limbs glisten and sparkle. Even the weather was beautiful. Maybe she just needed to relax. She turned back to Rachel. "It's not that I don't understand it. I'm just surprised there's no crisis to deal with."

Rachel came to the table with mugs of hot chocolate for each of them and sat down.

"Isn't it great? Other than that minor hiccup with the seats, it's been smooth sailing. Everybody we hired finished their portion of the job on time. I think that's a minor miracle right there."

Maura nodded, wrapping her hands around the warm mug. "This is the first time I've done any remodeling myself, but on those TV shows the crew always goes over schedule and over budget. Which reminds me, how is our budget?"

Rachel shuffled through the papers until she found the right spreadsheet. "Good." She pushed the sheet across the table to Maura. "We did go over just a smidge in a few places. But my financial genius husband planned ahead for that and built in some wiggle room. Overall, we're doing great."

"Now we just have to keep it that way." She looked at Rachel over the rim of her mug. "We've got to start bringing in revenue."

Rachel nodded. "I've been thinking about that. Since we'll be ready for business after the first of December, why don't we have some screenings of old movies with Christmas themes?"

Maura sat up straighter in her chair. "Ooh, I like it. We could show *White Christmas* and *It's a Wonderful Life*." Just saying the titles made her feel nostalgic.

They spent the next half hour talking about contacting film distributors, advertising, and spreading the word about the theatre/meeting center beyond the boundaries of Granger.

"And don't forget," Rachel said, "we've got to put together that Christmas pageant with Faith."

How could she possibly forget? "Got it covered. Lainie and I already started working on it. We've got the youth doing a couple of skits, and the Sunday school kids singing some carols. I still need to flesh it out a bit, though. You wouldn't happen to know any people with amazing hidden talents, would you?"

"I'll give it some thought. But what about Nick?"

"What about him?"

"Just that you haven't mentioned him. Since this is a joint project with the church, I assumed he'd be involved. Do you have a part for him?"

That was a loaded question. Ever since he came to her rescue with the men's breakfast group, she'd found herself thinking of Nick and what part they would play in each other's lives. It was as though some huge barrier had been torn down, and Maura could actually imagine a time when they might be able to repair their broken relationship and live as husband and wife again. But some doubt still lingered. Even though she'd forgiven Nick, she hadn't been able to forget the pain of needing him and having him choose the church over her. And she was scared to death that if she gave him the chance, he'd do it again.

"Sure, there's a part for him in the gala," she said, answering Rachel's question. "He's the master of ceremonies. He'll kind of narrate it all and move us from group to group."

"Great. It looks like everything is under control and we can consider this meeting adjourned." Rachel began to gather up all the papers, putting them away neatly in file folders. "There's just one more thing we have to talk about."

"What's that?"

"Have you thought about Thanksgiving?"

Oh, she'd thought about it, all right. It was just a week away, and she'd been mulling over the idea of cooking dinner for Nick. Sadly, her talents did not lie in the cooking department. The prospect of picking out a turkey, let alone cleaning it, stuffing it, and roasting it, was daunting.

Maura wrinkled her nose. "I've been trying not to think about cooking, but I guess it's time I Googled some turkey recipes."

"Don't bother. I want you to join us for Thanksgiving dinner. Nick too." Rachel held up her hand before Maura could reply. "Think about how perfect it'll be. You won't have to bother with a big, fancy dinner for the two of you, but you'll get to spend a holiday together. And being here, there will be less pressure for you both."

Why had Maura thought she could keep Rachel in the dark? "Just how did you figure out that Nick and I even want to be together?"

"I saw it the day of the infamous seat harvest, and you've been acting different ever since. You've been walking around like there are springs in your shoes, and he's been happy and whistling all the time." Rachel shrugged. "The signs are there, if you know where to look. Most people don't look."

Maura laughed. "I'm glad you're on my side."

"You know it. So, what do you think about my invitation?"

"I think it's great. Let me talk to Nick, and I'll let you know for sure."

"Sounds good. Oh, and one more thing." Rachel put her hand on Maura's, giving it a gentle squeeze. "If you think there's a chance for reconciliation, and I certainly am rooting for that, you might want to start letting people see the two of you together as a couple. It'll be good for everyone concerned."

So much had changed in just four months.

Maura stepped into the theatre, pride surging through her. It was a far cry from the place she'd first walked into. All the dust and dirt was gone. Instead of an unused, neglected theatre, the Music Box had been restored to its former glory. Maura had tried to remain as true to the original décor as possible, and the results were truly impressive.

She climbed up the steps to the stage and looked out over the clean, bright carpeting that covered the aisles, the newly varnished wood floor that was ready and waiting for the installation of the freshly reupholstered seats. She'd accomplished so much in such a short period of time.

But her mind kept returning to her conversation with Rachel.

Could this be the right time to make her changing relationship with Nick public knowledge? If they kept moving forward, there was a good possibility they would get back together. If Maura only had herself and Nick to consider, the next step would be easier. But if she stepped back into her role as Nick's wife, as a pastor's wife, she'd have the congregation to deal with again. Was she ready for that?

But maybe that's what Rachel meant. Maura had already become more visible in the congregation. People saw her working with the youth and knew about the theatre project. While she redefined her identity in the eyes of the congregation, she was also setting down clear boundaries. If she let them see her with Nick, and they realized that he supported her, it might make the transition easier if she and Nick were able to completely reunite.

Maura glanced down at her watch. She had a meeting in fifteen minutes with a graphic designer to discuss promotional materials and logo design. At the moment, there was nothing more she could do about her situation with Nick. She'd put it out of her mind for now, but they'd definitely talk about it tonight. He'd promised to make dinner for them both, and now that she had a plan, she was looking forward to it more than ever.

Nick hurried up the front porch stairs, carefully avoiding icy patches as he went. What a day it had been. He'd jumped from one crisis to the next, and found himself alternating between prayer and counting. Finally, his official work came to an end. At five o'clock he'd packed up and was ready to leave the office. All he had to do was walk next door, and he'd be home. Just as his hand touched the doorknob, the phone call came.

It wasn't the first time he'd had to drop everything to help this family. In fact, he'd been on his way to their remote farm the day Maura left him. She'd called on his cell phone, but the reception was so bad, he'd only been able to understand part of what she said. Something about not feeling well and wanting him to come home. He'd told her to eat some soup, get some rest, and he'd be there as soon as he could. Then the line went dead. And when he'd gotten home, she was gone.

He came to a dead stop in front of the parsonage door. He'd done it again. He should have called Maura to tell her about the emergency. At least she could have made other plans for dinner. But he'd been so focused on what needed to be done at the time, he hadn't thought of anything else.

Nick opened the door, not sure what awaited him on the other side.

He found her at the kitchen sink with her back to him. Music poured from the portable CD player on the counter. Maura hummed along as she rinsed off the dishes and loaded the dishwasher. Wearing simple jeans and a big sweatshirt with the sleeves pushed to her elbows, she was the prettiest sight he'd seen all day.

How he'd missed this . . . missed her. Yes, he found great fulfillment in his work, and he knew for a fact it was what God had called him to do. But without someone to share it with, without someone to come home to, he lived a life as hollow as that big empty theatre after all the seats were gone.

That day had been a real turning point. The constant tension that existed between them since Maura's return had gone, replaced by the excitement of getting reacquainted. He just hoped he hadn't blown it. Again.

"I'm so sorry." Probably not the best opening line, but it was the first thing that came to mind. And he did mean it.

She looked over her shoulder. "Oh, you're home. There's a plate for you in the fridge if you're hungry. Nothing special. I just scrounged up some leftovers. But you can pop it in the microwave if you want."

Nick wasn't sure how to read the situation. She wasn't yelling at him, which was good, but she didn't look particularly happy, either. Her voice came out flat, not hinting at any emotion. Opening the refrigerator door, he took out the plate she'd fixed for him.

"How long should I heat this?"

Maura loaded the last cup and shut the dishwasher door. "Here," she said, drying her hands on a towel. "Let me."

Nick watched her take the plate to the microwave. She sounded calm and pleasant, but she shut the microwave door a little too firmly and punched the timer buttons on the front panel with a little too much enthusiasm.

Uh oh.

"Maura, I'm so sorry about dinner," he said again. "There was an emergency with a member of the congregation. I had to take care of it. Do you understand?"

She leaned her hips against the side of the counter, her arms crossed in front of her. "Nick, I know you're a pastor. And over the last month, I've finally taken a good, hard look at what that means. I know you love people, and you need to take care of them. It's built into your nature. So, yes, I do understand. But, I don't think you understand."

"What?"

She jabbed at her chest. "Yes, the congregation needs you. But so do I. When it gets right down to it, I'm also a member of your congregation now, and sometimes, I need you just as much as they do. Not only as a husband, but as my pastor."

He hadn't expected this. "I'm sorry, Maura. I know I should have called and told you I'd be home late. But the call tonight was quite literally a life and death matter."

She tilted her head to one side, her eyes narrowed. "Don't you think you're being a little overdramatic?"

"No, I'm not." He struggled to keep himself calm, reminding himself she had no idea why he'd stood her up. "I responded to a suicide attempt. I can't discuss the details, but I've been working with this person for years and I've never seen it as bad as today."

Maura deflated. Her shoulders drooped, and she stared at the floor. "That's terrible. And definitely more important than dinner." She looked back up at him. "But I'm not just talking about tonight. I understand missing dinner, although you're right about calling. You should have."

"Then what are you talking about?"

"There have been times in the past when I needed you, really needed you to support me and to comfort me, and you weren't there." Her voice broke, and Nick could see her fight to control her emotions. "I've forgiven you for the past. I was hoping we could move forward and maybe fix our relationship. I was this close." She held her thumb and fingers so close together he could barely see light between them. "This close to trusting you again. But today just reminded me of how much it hurts to be forgotten. And I don't know if I can open myself up for that again."

The bell on the microwave timer sounded, but they both ignored it. Something else stood between them. Something she wasn't telling him. Nick wanted to beg her to talk about it since it was probably what had motivated her to leave him. But this was no time to grill her. He stepped closer to Maura and took her hands in his.

"You're right about who I am. God called me here to this church and it's my duty to love the people and take care of them. But God also called me to be your husband, and that means I need to love and care for you too. I'm so sorry that I hurt you."

"I know you're sorry. But does that mean anything will change?"

"I'm telling you now that I intend to be more sensitive to your needs. I promise to do the best I can. But I'm just a man. I'll make mistakes. And you need to realize there will be times, like tonight, when I have no choice but to go where I'm needed. Like it or not, I don't have a clear-cut, nine-to-five job."

He took a chance pointing this out, but they had to address the issue. They'd married so fast and moved out to Granger on a burst of excitement. Not once had they talked through the reality of what their life would be like. They needed to have that conversation now. They both made mistakes, and they both needed to bend. He just hoped Maura saw it the same way.

Finally, she nodded. "I need to take this slow. And I can't promise you anything. But I think I see a whole lot of prayer in my future." She glanced over at the microwave. "Your food's getting cold."

He shrugged. "I can always nuke it again." He pulled her into his arms and hugged her, wishing that simple act could heal the wounds she carried with her.

12

Quiet down, everybody! I've got a few announcements before I set you loose on society."

Lainie stood at the front of the youth room, one arm raised high in the air. Most of the teens stopped what they were doing and gave her their attention. Standing in her usual corner at the back of the room, Maura once again marveled at Lainie's control over this energetic bunch.

"Thank you," she said once the group settled down. "First off, I want to remind you that Thanksgiving is a great time to invite friends to church. And to make it even easier, I made up some invitations." She crooked her finger at one of the girls in the front row. "Sarah, would you hand these out, please?"

Sarah took the box Lainie handed her and started walking around the room.

"Take as many as you think you'll need," Lainie continued. "I can always print up more if we run out. As you can see, they're business cards with the church address, website, and service times. This way, you can invite somebody and just give them the card. Very low key. Very low pressure."

When Sarah reached her, Maura took one of the cards. What a great idea. It would be much easier to invite a friend if you didn't have to worry about rattling off all the details like time and location. The card took care of all that.

"One last thing," Lainie said from the front. "Even if you're new in town, like me, I'm sure you know about the Founders' Day Carnival by now. It's the day after Thanksgiving, and we're blessed to have a booth there. It'll be a great fundraiser for us, but only if we have enough people to work it. So if you haven't already, make sure you sign up for a shift on your way out."

Nobody moved. Lainie grinned and waved her hands toward the door. "That means I'm done. Leave. Be gone. Be blessed."

The room emptied with amazing speed, leaving Lainie and Maura surrounded by the usual mess.

"Have you ever considered making them help clean up before they leave?" Maura asked as she took the vacuum out of the closet.

"I did once, for about a minute. But my time with them is so short, I hate to use any of it on boring stuff like cleaning." She tossed two huge throw pillows into a corner. "Besides, this gives us an opportunity to work on our servant's hearts."

Maura smirked. "Just what I need. Another opportunity."

"Speaking of which, would you be interested in helping with our fundraiser?"

Maura hesitated. "What would I have to do?"

"Supervise, mostly. I want a couple of kids in the booth at all times so folks can see who they're contributing to. But I also need an adult to make sure it all runs smoothly. So what do you say? Are you ready to take a shift in the Kiss booth?"

Maura stopped the vacuum in mid-push. "Kissing booth? What are you trying to teach these kids?"

Lainie crossed her arms, her head cocked to the side. "I thought you knew me better than that. I didn't say *kissing* booth, I said *Kiss* booth. As in Hershey's Kisses."

"Oh, the chocolate kind."

"Yes. There will be three wicker baskets at the back of the booth. For a dollar, you get to throw three softballs, and if you get one in a basket, you win a small bag of chocolate Kisses."

Maura continued her vacuuming. "You had me worried for minute. I never should have doubted you."

Lainie laughed. "I should say not. Although, I've gotten that same reaction from everyone who hears the name, which is exactly what I hoped for. It's all part of creating word-of-mouth interest and driving customers to our booth."

"Now you sound like a marketing expert."

Lainie grabbed up a bottle of cleaner and spritzed it on the white board. "My daddy's a professor," she said offhandedly. "He teaches marketing and business theory. I guess after hearing him talk for so many years, I picked up some of the lingo."

Maura pulled the cord out of the way and maneuvered the vacuum into a corner. "I've never heard you talk about your parents before. Are you spending Thanksgiving with them?"

Lainie cleaned the board with one final, decisive wipe. When she turned, her usually perky demeanor had turned serious. "No, we don't see each other very much anymore."

"Why not?"

"It's a long story, but I'll give you the condensed version. They didn't agree with my choice to become a youth leader." Lainie snorted. "Actually, it goes farther back than that. They didn't agree with my choice of becoming a Christian."

A pang of sadness shot through Maura. No matter how hard her life had been she'd always been secure in her father's love and support, even when he didn't agree with her choices. She turned off the vacuum and wheeled it back to the closet. How terrible for Lainie to know her parents were opposed to the most important part of who she was.

Lainie shrugged. "I'm not upset about it anymore, but it's too hard to be with them, knowing how they feel. And it makes me sad to think what's missing in their lives. So I just pray for them, and go on doing what I do." She forced a smile. "What about you? Will you spend Thanksgiving with your parents?"

Maura shook her head. "No. My mother died of breast cancer when I was sixteen. And my Da, that's my dad, passed away about six months ago."

"I'm sorry." Lainie paused. "Why do you call him Da?"

"It's what Irish kids call their dads."

"So you're full-blooded Irish?"

"Half. My mother was American. The two of them met when she came to Ireland one summer to visit her cousins."

Lainie put her palm to her chest. "How romantic."

"You don't know the half of it," Maura said with a chuckle. "This is how Da liked to tell the story. It was the beginning of summer, and he was working on his father's farm like he always did, driving a wagon down the same road he always drove down, not expecting anything out of the ordinary, when he spied her. He called her a vision from a dream, riding her bicycle on the side of the road, coming toward him. When he got close enough, he tipped his hat. The vision smiled at him. He passed her, but couldn't help looking back, just to make sure he hadn't imagined her. And when he did, she was looking back too. Which is why she ran off the road."

"No!" Lainie gasped.

"Yes. She ran her bike right into a ditch." As always, the image of her solid-as-a-rock mother being so googly-eyed over a boy that she ended up in a ditch got Maura laughing.

"That's priceless," Lainie said, laughing along with her. "So it must have been love at first sight."

"Yep. They really loved each other." Maura dabbed at the tears that were a mixture of joy in the story and pain from the loss of her parents. "I miss them. But at least now they're together."

Lainie threw her arm around Maura's shoulder and gave her a quick squeeze. "Thanks for sharing that story with me. It does my heart good to know some people are like that. But since you're not spending Thanksgiving with family, what are you doing?"

"Rachel Nelson invited me to have dinner with her family. Hey, why don't you join us?" The request came out of her mouth at the same time she thought it. Normally, she didn't go around inviting people to someone else's home, but she knew Rachel wouldn't mind setting a place for one more.

"That's sweet of you, but I couldn't."

"Why not? Nick will be there too."

Lainie's eyebrows shot up. "No kidding? Does that mean you two are getting serious?"

Maura smiled. Lainie certainly knew how to get to the point. "To be honest, I don't know what it means. We're still working through some issues."

Lainie nodded. "Trust God. He'll fix whatever's broken. You know, I've been praying for the two of you since the day I met you."

It seemed like a million years ago when Maura had walked back into Granger with a chip on her shoulder the size of the Rockies. "I was jealous of you that day I saw you with Nick at the house," she confessed.

"Of me? Why?"

"I thought you and Nick might be an item."

"Me and Pastor Nick? Ewww!" Lainie wrinkled her nose and jumped backward, looking like one of the teenagers she led. "Nick's like my big brother. Wow, was your radar off! Besides, there's no way he'd ever date anyone else as long as he's married to you."

"True." Maura's cheeks flushed. The conversation was getting a little too personal. "But we've gotten off track here. What do you say about Thanksgiving dinner? Will you come?"

"You talked me into it."

Lainie picked up her purse and Bible. They walked to the door together, and Lainie giggled as she snapped off the lights.

"What's so funny?" Maura asked.

"I was just thinking, considering the way you and I started out, it's amazing how God knit us together. Not only are we friends, He made you my assistant youth director."

Maura stopped short. On her first go-round at Faith Community, people had tried to hand her all kinds of titles: Sunday school director, Hospitality Hostess, Women's Ministry Liaison. Every one of them had tied up her stomach in knots.

Assistant youth director. She rolled the words around in her head. With a grin, she followed Lainie out of the room.

It worked for her.

13

Thanksgiving turned out far better than Nick could have hoped. After standing up Maura for dinner the previous week, he thought he'd blown any chance of reconciliation. But she surprised him by inviting him to join her for Thanksgiving dinner at the Nelsons. She shocked him even more when she said she'd invited Lainie as well. It was good to know Maura didn't have any more concerns about him and the youth director.

Rachel made a turkey dinner so good it would make a Pilgrim weep. Lainie provided chocolate cupcakes to supplement the traditional pumpkin pie, eliciting cheers from Ben and Becca. They ate dessert in the living room where the conversation somehow turned to dating. Lainie wanted to know how Derrick and Rachel met. After a hilarious story about Rachel accidentally dumping a jumbo soda on Derrick at a monster truck rally, the conversation took an inevitable turn.

"No offense, Mom," Becca said, "but I've heard that story a million times. What I want to know is how did Maura and Pastor Nick meet?"

Everyone in the room looked at Maura, including Nick. How would she respond to this?

"Why are you all looking at me?" she said with a laugh. "Nick was there too." She smiled at him and gave him a nudge. "Go on. I want to hear how you remember it."

He cleared his throat. "Well, we were in college, and Maura worked as a waitress at her father's coffee shop. I came in a lot, but just because the chowder was so good."

"Oh, please," Maura said. "Nobody likes chowder that much. He came in all the time because he was checking me out."

Becca and Lainie giggled. Ben groaned. Derrick put his arm around Rachel.

Nick smiled. "Yes, I was. I wanted to ask her out, but she had a firm policy of never dating customers."

"Bad policy," Rachel said.

Maura shrugged.

Becca leaned forward in her seat. "But she gave in, right?"

Ben threw a pillow at his sister. "Well, duh. They're sitting together, aren't they?"

"It wasn't that easy," Nick said, waving his finger at them. "I had to find a way around her rule. So I did what any self-respecting gentleman would do. I vanquished a giant."

Lainie set her empty pie plate on the coffee table with a clunk. "You what?"

"I vanquished a giant."

Maura snorted. "I'd hardly call Butch a giant."

"He was six-nine if he was an inch."

She patted Nick's arm. "I think I'd better take it from here. What he did was challenge one of the regulars to a game of darts, and he got me to agree to go out with him if he won."

"Which I did," Nick said. Maura looked at him with her mouth quirked. "Okay, Butch was a sucker for young love, so I'm pretty sure he threw the game. But I still won."

Maura nodded. "Yes, you did. Which led to our first date. And the rest is history."

"Cool story," Derrick said. "Now who's up for Pictionary?"

Nick silently thanked Derrick for changing the subject before the kids could ask anymore pointed questions.

Becca, Lainie, and Maura faced off against Ben, Derrick, and Rachel. Maura's amazing adeptness at translating her team's swirls and squiggles clinched the victory for them. It was a rousing game and the perfect end to a great night.

"You continue to surprise me with your hidden skills," Nick told her when they returned to the parsonage.

"Is that right?" she asked with raised eyebrows. "Other than Pictionary, what skills are you talking about?"

"Taking on a renovation project for one thing. And your flair for drama. I mean, I always knew you enjoyed it, I just didn't know you had such a passion for it. And there's the way you've won over the kids in the youth group."

"That's not a skill," she said, dismissing his compliment with a twitch of her shoulder. "That's just getting to know people."

"Don't sell yourself short. Not everybody can find something to relate to with a room full of teenagers. Respecting them and earning their respect in return, that's something special."

"Maybe, which reminds me. On the way out of church on Sunday Lainie made some off-handed reference to me being her assistant youth director." She put her fists on her hips, and gave him a serious look. "You wouldn't know anything about that, would you?"

Nick raised his hands. "It wasn't me, I promise. But you have been spending a lot of time working with her, and I could see tonight how well you two get along. Maybe she was just planting a little seed."

"Maybe."

A smile lit up Maura's face, bringing a warm glow to Nick's heart. Funny, he never would have thought to suggest that she get involved with the youth ministry. But she seemed to be a natural. He'd discovered another new facet to his wife.

Standing in the middle of the living room, sharing such easy camaraderie, Nick wondered what to do next. He didn't want the day to end.

"Would you like some coffee? I can put on a pot."

"No, thanks," Maura said. "I'm pretty tired, and I've got an early morning tomorrow."

"You're not working at the theatre are you?"

"I probably should. But no, I'm helping Lainie get the youth group booth set up at the carnival. After that, I've got first shift."

Another surprise. Surely, Maura knew the whole town would show up for the celebration, yet she agreed to participate in a church-sponsored booth. Maybe this meant she was warming up to the idea of being an active part of the congregation.

"Too bad you're working," he said. "I hoped you'd be my date tomorrow."

Maura bit down on her lower lip. "Hmm, that's a problem, isn't it? Especially since I planned to ask you to escort me to the carnival after my shift is over. Would you mind waiting for me?"

I've been waiting for you for six years, and I didn't even know it. "I'd love to wait for you."

"Good. Stop by the booth at one o'clock, and I'll let you show me the sights." She moved toward him for a hug, he thought, but at the last minute she moved sideways and planted a kiss on his cheek.

As simple and chaste as the kiss was, it set his heart to pounding like a bongo drum. *I love you.* It danced through his head as she walked away from him, leaving him dazed and temporarily unable to speak.

"Maura, wait!" he finally called after her.

She stopped and turned in the open doorway, her look expectant. "Yes?"

"I . . . Uh, what booth will you be in?"

"The Kiss booth. Goodnight."

With a wave of her hand she went into the bedroom and closed the door. It wasn't until Nick was settled down into his own bed that he realized what she'd said.

"*Kissing* booth?"

Nick walked down the main street of town, his hands stuffed into the pockets of his jacket. A crisp breeze nipped at his cheeks, but the sun shown brightly and, if the weather forecaster was to be believed, there was no chance of rain or snow. You couldn't ask for a better day for a carnival.

Traffic barricades at either end of Main Street created an eight-block thoroughfare of exhibits, game booths, and food stalls. The street teemed with people. It seemed as though the entire congregation of Faith Community Church had shown up for the celebration. A preoccupied Nick nodded and exchanged hellos with nearly everyone he passed as he craned his neck first left then right, looking for the infamous Kissing Booth. He hoped he'd misunderstood Maura last night, or he'd have more than a little explaining to do at the next church council meeting.

Nick heard Maura before he saw her.

"Come on, folks, don't be shy! Everybody gets a kiss just for playing!"

He quickened his pace, jogging through the crowd until he stood in front of the infamous game. A burst of relieved breath whooshed out of him as he looked over the "Kiss Booth," which was decorated with foil-covered cardboard cutouts of Hershey's Kisses.

"Hey Sarah. Nathan." He greeted the teenagers who worked behind the counter. Maura stood in front, encouraging all who passed to try out the game.

Nick leaned over and whispered in her ear. "Thank goodness you're giving away chocolate kisses."

Her eyebrows raised in innocent surprise. "Why, Nick, how could you think we were giving away anything else? That would be downright scandalous."

Nick laughed. "I'm just glad I don't have to hold a disciplinary meeting on Monday." He turned back to the teenagers. "Tell me how this works."

After they explained the premise of the game, he took his wallet from his back pocket and pulled out a dollar. "So," he said, waving it in the air, "for a dollar I get three chances? What if I get all three balls in a basket?"

Sarah answered him. "You get a monster Kiss." She pulled a huge, one-pound chocolate candy from beneath the counter and set it down with a thunk.

"It's harder than it looks," Nathan warned. "No one's been able to do it yet."

Nick picked up one of the balls. "That's because I haven't played yet."

He took aim and tossed the softball at the basket in front of him. It hit the center, but immediately bounced up and out over the low rim.

"Definitely harder than it looks," Nick said with a frown.

"They bounce," Maura managed to squeak out past her laughter.

Two minutes later, with his wallet ten dollars lighter, Nick still hadn't managed to get a ball to stay in a basket. But he had drawn a crowd to the booth. He tried throwing overhand, underhand, and sideways. He even closed his eyes once, and for the final ball, he turned his back to the baskets and tossed it over his shoulder, which produced a grunt from behind him.

"Sorry, Nathan," he said, turning around.

The teenager grinned as he rubbed his shoulder. "You really suck at this, Pastor Nick."

He laughed and nodded his head. "That I do, Nathan. That I do."

"But that's okay because everyone's a winner!" Maura cheered, which brought a round of applause from the group that had stopped to watch. She went back behind the booth and leaned over the counter toward Nick. "You get one Kiss for every dollar you donated."

"Great." He leaned in toward her so they were almost nose to nose. "That's ten kisses. Are you going to give them to me?"

"I sure am. Close your eyes and give me your hand."

With his eyes closed Nick became unusually aware of the sounds around him. Or rather, the lack of sounds. It seemed much quieter now as everyone waited to see just what would happen with the pastor and his wayward wife.

Maura's soft fingers closed around his hand, turning it palm up and spreading it open. "Here you go," she whispered.

When he opened his eyes, he held a small bag of brightly wrapped candies. Nick grinned. "Thank you, Maura. Especially for giving me these Kisses in public." He turned to the crowd who now laughed good-naturedly at him. "Who wants to give this a try and show me up?"

A flurry of dollar-wielding hands shot up, anxious for their chance to outdo the pastor. Lainie skirted her way around the mass of people and bounded up to the booth.

"Wow, what a response." She nudged Maura with her elbow. "You're a natural. Maybe I should just leave you here."

Maura snatched her purse from under the counter and ran around to the front of the booth. "No way. I've got a date."

Her choice of words caught Nick off guard, but he was really thrown when she linked her arm through his.

Lainie's smile grew broader. "Fair enough. Thanks for all your help. Now scoot, you two. Have fun."

They walked down the street together, admiring the different displays. When Maura spotted a hot dog vendor, she pulled them both up short and took a deep breath.

"That smells heavenly."

"It's just hot dogs."

"I haven't had anything to eat since breakfast, and I'm starving. Besides," she said, tugging on his hand, "sometimes nothing hits the spot like a street dog."

"Well, let's get you fed." He ordered a hot dog, chips, and a drink for each of them, which they carried to the picnic tables in the park.

"You sure are a cheap date," he said as they sat down.

She ignored the comment and bit into the hot dog, groaning in delight.

"So," Nick said as he opened his bag of chips, "does this mean you've forgiven me for being an inconsiderate boob last week?"

She must have been in mid-swallow, because she turned away and pounded her chest with her palm to stop her coughing fit.

Nick jumped up and leaned across the table. "You okay?"

She held up her hand and took a drink of her soda. "I'm fine," she choked out. "You just took me by surprise."

"I figured that out." He sat back down, trying to keep his face serious.

Maura wiped the corners of her mouth with a napkin. "Yes, I've forgiven you. And I never called you a boob."

He held a chip in the air. "But you thought it."

She tilted her head, as if recalling that day, then shook it sharply. "Nope. It never crossed my mind. Seriously, though, I have been thinking about us. A lot."

"What have you been thinking?"

"That if we're serious about trying to work things out, it's probably good for people to get used to seeing us together again. Is that okay?"

Is that okay? He'd wanted little more since she moved back into his house and worked her way back into his heart. If only she told him she was ready to be his wife again, in every sense of the word, the moment would be perfect. But he knew better than to bring that up so soon.

"It's great," he said, picking up his hot dog. "This is without a doubt the best Thanksgiving weekend I've had since we moved to Granger."

Maura's eyelids drooped, and she looked down at the table. "Do you realize this is our first Thanksgiving together?"

She was right. Theirs had been a whirlwind romance. He'd met her in March. They'd married in early June, right before coming to Granger, and had only lived in the town for about five months before their marriage went bad and she left. They'd never shared Thanksgiving or the Founders' Day celebration. They'd never spent a Christmas together, or even exchanged gifts.

"It looks like we're in for a season of firsts, huh?"

They finished their lunch, and Nick threw out the empty wrappers, cups, and napkins.

"Thank you," Maura said quietly.

"No problem. Got to do what we can to keep the town clean."

She shook her head. "No, I mean for being so nice about everything. You know, between us. We both made mistakes, but the way I left was wrong. I should have talked to you long before it got so bad. I should have told you . . . Anyway, thank you for giving me, us, a second chance."

Her mouth tugged down at one corner, and she looked like she was about to cry. Surrounded as they were by music and laughter, it seemed an odd place to have this conversation. But hope sprung up in Nick's heart.

He cupped his hand around her cheek. "I've thanked God every day since you came back. Well, almost every day. There were a few days there when you got on my last nerve."

They both laughed. "I'm sure you counted to ten more than once," Maura said.

"You could say that. But I'm not easy to live with, either. Whatever you didn't tell me before, I must have made you feel that you couldn't. I'm thankful for the second chance too."

Nick felt like a man who'd thawed out after being rescued from a snow storm. Every fiber of his body longed to hold her, to pull her close, and show her just how much he'd missed her. He wanted to ignore that they were in public and give the citizens of Granger something juicy to talk about. Instead, he kissed her on the forehead and drew her to him for a chaste hug.

She looked up at him, eyes warm and expectant. "What now?"

With one arm around her waist he led her out of the park and back toward the bustle of the carnival. "Now we'll find a booth where I can actually win you a prize."

14

This is it," Nick said as soon as he saw the Kill the Computer Virus booth. "You know how good I am with darts."

Maura winced. "Oh, yeah, I remember."

Alice, the Dot Spot employee working the booth, knew Maura well from her daily coffee runs. "Don't worry, you'll get a prize even if he doesn't hit anything."

Nick plunked down a dollar. "Why is everyone so sure I'll need the consolation prize? Now hand over those darts and tell me how this works."

Alice laid three darts on the counter in front of him. "It's simple. Throw a dart, break a balloon, and find the computer virus."

Nick picked up the first dart, taking careful aim. He let it fly, and it stuck in the board between two tightly packed balloons.

"Too bad the idea's not to leave the balloons intact," Maura said. "That takes some real talent."

"The first I've seen today," Alice agreed, holding back her laughter.

Nick ignored both of them. "I'm just getting warmed up. This one's a winner."

The next dart did hit a balloon, but it glanced off and fell to the ground.

"It bounced off," Nick said in amazement. "How does a dart hit a balloon and not break it? What are they made out of, Kevlar?"

Alice shook her head. "Nope, they're standard issue balloons. But they're under-inflated. It makes the game more challenging."

Nick nodded. "I see. That's okay." He picked up the last dart and rolled it between his fingers. "I have a long-standing history with darts, and the third time has always been the charm." He looked at Maura, his mouth lifted up in a crooked grin, and winked at her. "Isn't that right?"

How could she forget the time he'd come into her father's coffee shop and "vanquished" big old Butch so he could take her out on a date? The Nick she knew back then had been spontaneous and went out of his way to spend time with her and make her feel special. A delicious warmth flowed through her body, despite the winter chill.

Nick held up the dart and closed his eyes for a moment. He moved his hand back and forth, as if making up his own throwing rhythm. He took a deep breath, opened his eyes and sent the dart on its way.

It headed for the center of the board, but arced sharply down. It looked like it would drill straight into the booth's plywood floor, but at the last minute it caught the balloon at the left-hand bottom corner of the board.

Maura let out a shriek as the balloon exploded.

"You did it!" She threw her arms around Nick's neck.

He laughed as he returned the hug.

"Well, lookie there," Alice said. "Not only did you break a balloon, you managed to find one of the bugs. You killed the computer virus!"

Nick and Maura broke from the hug and looked back at the board. Sure enough, beneath the pieces of ragged latex they saw a picture of a cartoon bug lying on its back, feet in the air, next to a tombstone marked "R.I.P."

Maura patted Nick on the back. "Ooh, now I'm really impressed."

"Don't be. I aimed for the middle."

Alice took on a philosophical tone. "In this booth, as in life, intentions don't mean much. It's the results that count." She pointed to either side of the booth where samples of the big prizes were displayed. "Since the lady always does the choosing, which would you like, Maura? A gorilla or a tiger?"

They left the booth a minute later, a stuffed white tiger under Maura's arm. As they walked, they were constantly greeted by folks who wanted to say hello, or tell Nick how good the Thanksgiving message had been. It was the kind of interruption that had driven Maura crazy when she and Nick first moved to Granger. They couldn't go anywhere without people stopping Nick to talk about church business or to ask him about a personal problem. When it happened, Maura inevitably ended up standing off to the side, feeling awkward and ignored.

But now, their roles were different. Since Maura had become a presence in the community and the church, just as many people came up to say hello to her as they did to Nick. There were even a few people with whom she'd worked on the theatre project who hadn't met Nick before, so she was able to introduce them. Rather than feeling like she was floundering and forgotten, Maura felt like she was part of something.

She was part of the community.

"Wow, the place looks great."

"What?" Maura pushed her thoughts away and paid attention to where they were. They stood on the sidewalk in front of the theatre.

Nick admired the building. "I said it looks great. I go by here almost every day, but I still can't get over how you revived the old place."

The Music Box Theatre sparkled in the late afternoon sunlight. The display windows were spotless, and the brass around the ticket taker's booth had been polished till it shone. Big, bold letters on the marquee announced the grand opening on December 1, and replicas of vintage movie posters for a revival showing of *It's a Wonderful Life* hung in the "Now Showing" cases.

Nick walked up to one of the display windows that held posters, detailing upcoming events and group services that could be provided at the Music Box.

"The graphics on these are terrific." He motioned at the poster with his thumb. "And I saw one of your brochures at the house. I've got to say, I'm impressed. I had no idea you could do all this."

"Thanks, but I can't take credit for the print ads. My only talent there is in hiring great people," Maura said. "Pamela Schwaab did all the graphic design work."

"Bettie's granddaughter?"

Maura nodded. "The same. You look surprised."

"I am." He stuffed his hands in his jacket pockets, cocking his head to the side. "Don't get me wrong, Pam's a sweet girl, but she's a little . . ."

"Quiet?"

"Well, yes. Aren't artistic people usually more loud and flamboyant?"

"I guess. But now you're generalizing. You know you can't judge someone by their outward appearance."

"Ouch." Nick winced, his reaction overdone and comical. "Maybe you should take over the pulpit next Sunday."

Maura waved her hands in front of her. "Oh, no, buddy, not on your life. The last thing I need is to be a pastor."

"Agreed. Besides, between me and Chris, we don't need another pastor. But," he added quietly, "we could use a pastor's wife."

Maura narrowed her eyes. "We? As in, the congregation needs you to have a wife?"

"The congregation would like me to have a wife. But I need one. To be more specific, I need you." He took a step closer to Maura and put his hand on her waist. "So what do you think? Could 'pastor's wife' fit into your job description?"

Job description. Boy, he'd gotten that right. Maura had learned that being married to a pastor did bring with it some job-like aspects. That knowledge gave her a certain amount of power. Knowing what to expect, and what others expected from her, equipped her to deal with it. From that perspective, being a pastor's wife didn't seem as daunting as it once had. But the crux of the problem stood in front of her: Nick himself. She loved him. There had never been any doubt about that. And she believed he truly did love her. But if she agreed and they got back together, would love be enough to sustain her during those times when it felt like everyone in the congregation came first?

"I think it's a strong possibility," she finally answered him. "But I want to take it slow and make sure we're both absolutely certain of what we're committing to. For right now, how about we enjoy our date?"

She could tell Nick had hoped for a more decisive answer. But he had the good grace to smile and nod politely.

"You know how I feel," he said, "so for now I'll leave the ball in your court. If you decide you're ready to move our relationship along, you just let me know." He slipped his arm around her waist and led her away from the theatre.

As they walked down the street, Maura let herself relax. Now that Nick had given her the time she needed, she could concentrate on fulfilling the stipulations of Miss Hattie's will. But thinking about that made her tense up again. Her calendar was so full she hardly had a blank spot on it. Between the Music Box's grand reopening in a little over a week, rolling out drama classes, rehearsing the Christmas program, and working with the youth group, Maura saw little free time on the horizon. Somehow, she had to find a way to pencil in time to reconnect with Nick.

And there was the matter of what to do when she completed her time at the parsonage. At the end of January, the six months would be up, the deed to the Music Box would be hers free and clear, and she could live wherever she wanted. At that point she'd need to make a decision, one way or another.

They walked around the corner, and Maura came to an abrupt halt, jerking Nick to a stop. "Whoa! I didn't know anyone sprung for rides at this shindig."

Nick laughed. "Well, sure. The bank always sponsors a Ferris wheel. It's our only ride, but it's a classic."

Sure enough, there stood the enormous wheel in the parking lot of the Granger Savings and Loan. From the length of the line snaking away from the ticket taker up front, it appeared to be quite popular.

"What do you say?" he asked. "You feeling brave?"

Maura looked from Nick to the wheel towering above them. She'd never been crazy about heights.

She looked back at Nick. "Is it safe?"

"No, we just figure it's good for everyone's prayer life if we set up a death trap now and then." Nick shook his head. "Of course, it's safe. Would I even ask you to ride if it wasn't?"

Maura put a hand on her hip. "Just for that, I should walk off and leave you here."

Nick immediately looked contrite. "You're right. I'm sorry." He fell to one knee, held his hands up to her and wailed melodramatically, "Can you ever forgive me, sweet Maura?"

"Stop that!" Maura smacked him in the shoulder with the head of her stuffed tiger. "Get up before somebody sees you and gets the wrong idea." She'd already noticed a couple of the teens from the youth group elbowing each other and pointing.

Nick rose to his feet, grinning widely. "Seriously, riding a Ferris wheel is practically a required activity for a courting couple. So, will you do me the honor?"

Hearing him call them a courting couple made her heart melt like a chocolate kiss in the sun. He was making such an effort to woo her. At least she could conquer her fear of heights and go along with it.

"Okay," she gulped. "I'll give it a whirl."

The line moved much faster than she'd hoped. Before she knew it, they were greeted by Herb Munson, the bank manager. "Good to see you, Pastor. And Maura, you look lovely as ever. Glad to see you two out and about."

Nick returned the greeting, handed him their tickets, and boarded the ride. Maura sat beside him and gasped as the seat swayed several inches.

"Is it supposed to do that?" she asked Herb.

"Of course," he said as he locked the safety bar in place. "If the seat didn't move, you'd be upside down by the time you got to the top."

"Upside down!"

Nick put his hand on Maura's, which gripped the bar in front of her so tightly that her knuckles had turned white. "Relax," he told her. "This is supposed to be fun."

"Uh huh," she squeaked out.

Nick shook his head. "You grew up at the beach. Haven't you ever been on a boardwalk Ferris wheel before?"

"No, Da didn't take us to any of the beachside amusement areas. Said he didn't like the element. We went to Disneyland a few times, but they didn't have a Ferris wheel back then."

"Do they have one now?"

Maura nodded, but that small movement made the seat move again, so she froze and stared straight ahead. "Uh huh. At California Adventure. It's huge. Never been on it, either."

The wheel lurched forward. With a yelp, Maura fell back in the seat. She released the bar, and grabbed the first object she could find, which happened to be Nick's arm. The wheel moved up a few feet before it stopped again.

"Did the ride break?" Maura asked as their seat swayed.

"No. We'll stop like this until the ride's full. Then we'll go around a few times. While the ride empties out, we'll go back to the stop and start thing. Are you going to be okay?" He leaned over the edge of the seat and studied the ground with no fear at all. "We're not too far up yet. We could probably still jump out and not break anything."

She was pretty sure he was kidding, but didn't want to chance it. "No, I'll stay put. Thanks."

By the fourth time the wheel stopped to let on new passengers, Maura felt more comfortable with the ride. When it continued around in one smooth, slow arc, she even enjoyed it.

Somewhere along the way, Nick had put his arm around her shoulders She leaned into him, enjoying how solid and secure he felt. He smelled like Irish Spring soap, just like she remembered. Funny how a little detail like a scent could take you right back.

"This is nice," she said softly. "I'm glad you talked me into it."

Nick's arm squeezed her tightly. "Me too."

They were at the top of the wheel when it came to a stop once more. "I guess the ride's almost over," Maura said.

"Yep. Better take one last chance to admire the view."

The setting sun cast the sky in hues of pink, purple, and orange. Below them, the town of Granger had never looked prettier, or more like home.

The thought struck Maura in the pit of her stomach. When she'd returned to Granger, her one purpose had been to retrieve whatever Miss Hattie left her and beat it out of town. Once she'd discovered the stipulations of the will, she'd planned to carry them out so in six months' time she could sell the theatre, take the money, and leave. But gradually, her plans had changed. She'd come to like the idea of running the theatre, turning it into something that would not only bring her an income, but also benefit the community. And somewhere along the line, this small town had become her home.

No matter what happened between her and Nick, Granger would continue to be home. And that made everything look different.

"We're not moving."

"What?" Nick's statement pulled her back to the moment.

He frowned. "We should have moved by now."

They looked at each other, then looked down at the crowd standing by the ride operator. Maura recognized most of the people below them, including several members of the youth group.

"What's wrong?" Nick called.

Herb Munson cupped his hands around his mouth and called back. "You've got to kiss her!"

Nick did a double take. "What?"

"It's tradition," the bank manager boomed. "When you get to the top of the wheel, you've got to kiss your lady."

The growing crowd below them cheered and clapped. And to Maura's chagrin, they chanted, "Kiss! Kiss! Kiss!"

Her cheeks burned as she turned to Nick. "Did you put them up to this?"

"Trust me. I'm as surprised as you are."

From the car behind them came another voice. "Come on, Preacher, give her a smooch so we can all get down. I want to buy some cotton candy before they close up."

Nick laughed. "Well, how can we argue with that?" He looked down again before turning back to Maura. "I think we're outnumbered."

She nodded.

Nick pulled her closer. And there, in front of most of the town of Granger, with the sun setting behind them, Maura received her first kiss atop a Ferris wheel.

15

The weather could be a problem.

Maura and Rachel built up the grand reopening of the Music Box Theatre as a major event in the town of Granger. They sent out invitations and placed ads in the local paper. Everything was ready, from the big black letters spelling out GRAND OPENING on the marquee, to the bunting-draped podium that would stand outside the front doors, and the long tables full of hors d'oeuvres, coffee, and spiced cider ready to set up in the lobby. No detail had been overlooked

None except the possibility of a fast-moving winter storm.

Maura jumped out of bed and ran to the window, praying the snow that had fallen steadily for the last two days had stopped. No such luck. Not only did it continue to fall, but from the way the wind blew, it appeared to be coming in sideways.

She pursed her lips and glared out the window, as if the sheer force of her will could make the snow stop. She rolled her eyes upward and watched the fat flakes fall out of a leaden sky.

"God, I know I haven't talked to you much in the last few years. And now that I've started back up, I'm asking for a lot of favors. But I could sure use a break in the weather today. Around five o'clock, if that works for you."

As if an immediate answer to her prayer, the wind died down for a moment, but just as quickly another gust whipped the flakes into the frenzy of a cyclone.

Maura smiled as she walked away from the window. If only it were that easy.

She pulled open her dresser drawer and chose a black turtleneck. Despite the weather, a wonderful feeling of peace and satisfaction wrapped itself around her. She'd worked hard for this day, and she intended to enjoy it—even if she had to stand in a snowdrift to greet the four or five people who braved the elements to attend the opening.

When she finally stood in front of the theatre, warmth enveloped Maura despite the frigid wind biting her cheeks and nose. She never should have worried. The citizens of Granger were as predictable as the post office—neither sleet nor snow would keep them from attending a civic function, especially when it involved free food.

Maura jumped as Rachel dug an elbow into her ribs. "See, I told you people would show up. Curiosity trumps comfort every time."

Maura leaned closer to her friend, answering out of the corner of her mouth. "Still, we'd better move this along before we all freeze solid out here."

Saying another silent prayer of thanks that the former heavy snowfall had turned into barely there flurries, she pulled her coat closer around her and stepped up to the podium. "If I can have your attention!"

She waited as the people standing in front quieted down. One by one, they turned and shushed the people behind them. When she was confident everyone could hear, she continued.

"I'd like to thank you all for coming. This is truly a great day for me. For all of us. Before we cut the ribbon, I'd like to dedicate this theatre to the memory of Miss Hattie Granger." Applause rippled through the crowd. "She was quite a lady, and I can't thank her enough for believing in me and giving me the chance to restore this wonderful old building."

Maura looked out at the people gathered in front of the theatre, and something stirred in her chest, like the rapid flutter of hummingbird wings. She had spent so many years with her heart hardened toward this town and everybody in it. She'd seen them as adversaries, people who expected her to live up to a standard she couldn't achieve. But now, she saw them differently. Yes, they'd made assumptions about the kind of wife Maura should be, but she'd never stood up for herself. She'd made assumptions too, thinking they wouldn't accept the real her. Rather than talking to people and sharing her own goals and passions, she'd stuffed her feelings and tried to make everybody happy. In the end, she only made herself and everyone around her miserable.

A rumbling whisper moved through the crowd. They were impatient, hugging themselves tightly and stamping their feet to ward off the cold. She couldn't make them wait any longer. But she didn't know how to put into words all that she was feeling.

"I'd like to thank all the citizens of Granger," she blurted out. "For welcoming me back and giving me another chance to be a part of this community."

All noise and movement in the crowd stopped. Panic seized Maura. Had she misspoken? Maybe they weren't glad to have her back after all. Maybe they'd just been putting up with her in order to get their theatre back, and after the six months were over, they'd run her out of town.

But then a few people started clapping. Someone in the back whistled. Finally the rest of the crowd joined in, clapping and cheering.

Maura smiled as she batted snowflakes from her face. The skies had opened up again. As much as she'd like to stand there basking in the moment, she had to move the crowd inside soon. There was just one more thing to do before the ribbon cutting.

Where was Nick?

Maura scanned the crowd. She turned to Rachel, put her hands together as if in prayer and mouthed "Nick?" Rachel responded with a shrug of her shoulders. Turning back to the crowd, Maura searched each face, wondering if she was missing him beneath a hood or a scarf. He had to be there. He'd been so pleased last night when she asked him to say a blessing at the grand opening. He wouldn't stand her up today. Would he?

A different kind of movement stirred in the crowd. It began at the back, people sidestepping to clear a path and moving back into place. Maura slowly exhaled as Nick stepped up to the podium.

He stood beside her, pulling her into a quick, one-armed hug. "I think I speak for everyone here when I say it's good to have you back." Confirming his statement, the crowd erupted into a fresh round of applause. He leaned in closer and whispered, "Sorry I'm late. I had a heck of a time finding a parking place."

His breath warmed her cheek. Maura grinned up at him and squeezed his waist. Late she could handle. He made it, and that's what mattered. "Would you mind praying now, before we turn into popsicles?"

She felt the rumble of Nick's laugh, despite the many layers of winter-wear between them. He turned his attention to the crowd, holding up his hands.

"Okay, folks, it's cold out here, and I know we'd all like to get inside and check out the place. But we've got one more bit of business to attend to. Please join me in thanking the One who makes everything possible."

Maura bowed her head along with everyone else. As Nick thanked God for the blessings He'd given them, her heart joined in. *Thank you, Lord, for bringing me home, and bringing me back to You.*

"Amen," Nick said with gusto. He turned to Maura and winked. "You've got it from here."

Maura joined Rachel in front of a wide, red ribbon stretched across the front doors. With a grin splitting her face, Rachel handed her a huge pair of scissors.

"You've worked hard for this, girl," Rachel said. "Do the honors."

Maura embraced her friend and business partner, holding the scissors aside so as not to impale either of them. "*We've* worked hard. And this," she said, hoisting the scissors, "is big enough for both of us to grab a piece. Come on, let's do the honors together."

The two women cut the ribbon. The ends fluttered down and away, a startling contrast to the snow-covered ground where they landed. Maura and Rachel pulled the doors open and ushered their first visitors into the newly remodeled Music Box Theatre.

People rushed in, stomping their snowy boots on the door-mats. Some headed straight for the food tables set up in the lobby. Others looked around, eyes wide. Maura caught bits and pieces of conversation as people swirled past her.

"Can you believe this?"

"Look, they've got Jujubes in the candy counter!"

"It's even nicer than I remember it!"

Maura stripped off her coat, her mind spinning.

I love being part of a community.
I am so blessed.
I'll need to clean the carpet again.

After the successful grand opening of the refurbished theatre, Maura became busier than ever. Movie revival nights were well attended, and more than one group contacted her about renting out the facility. But the biggest and most unexpected hit was the acting classes.

Intrigued by the offer of a free first class, quite a few people signed up to try them out. So many, in fact, she had to split the group into two separate classes. It came as quite a surprise to see Oren Thacker's name on the list. She still didn't know him well, but she remembered his displeasure at the council meeting when she'd talked about the Christmas Gala. He probably wanted to check up on her and assess Granger's newest business. She certainly didn't expect him to have much aptitude for acting.

She was wrong.

At the first class, she went over some acting basics. and gave each student a short monologue. With a perverse sense of satisfaction she handed Oren the soliloquy from *Hamlet*. It wasn't really fair to assign Shakespeare on the first day, but Oren had been pretty hard on her the first time she'd been on his turf. Now she'd see if he could take as good as he gave.

Oren wasn't fazed when he took the scene. Minutes later, she knew why. His voice, which she'd never paid much attention to before, was rich and warm. As he read, he became the tortured prince of Denmark. His deep baritone found the subtle nuances in Shakespeare's English and took the class to a place far from their little town in Ohio. No one in the room made a sound as he spoke, and when he finished, they burst into applause. Oren shook his head, as if returning to the theatre from some other realm. A gentle, almost shy smile drew up the corners of his mouth, and his eyes sparkled with the joy that had so obviously been missing when they sat in the church meeting room.

Conviction poked Maura's heart. She'd never seen Oren express any emotion other than annoyance, so she'd assumed him incapable of feeling anything else. Obviously, her assessment was way off the mark. And if she'd been wrong about that, what else had she been wrong about? She'd let her hurt over the past color her perception of the present, keeping her from seeing the real Oren. How many other people had she treated the same way? It was an unpleasant realization.

After the class, she approached him privately. "Oren, you're amazing. Where did you learn to act?"

For the first time, Oren smiled directly at her. "I studied drama in college, but I had to give it up when my father fell ill. I came back to Granger and took over the hardware store. You could say I traded Shakespeare for sheetrock." He tried to joke it off, but regret tinged his words.

"Thacker and Sons Hardware is a long way from Broadway."

He nodded solemnly. "True, but it's been a good living. Allowed me to provide for my family. And look what God's done now. I never expected you to hold acting classes here. It takes me back to when I was a young man full of dreams."

Amazing! Maura's simple classes had resurrected Oren's dreams on the Music Box stage. "I hope you decide to stay in the class. Or maybe you should help me teach. You're certainly good enough."

Oren shook his head. "Oh, no, I want to be part of the class, at least for now. It's one way I can support the theatre and show you my appreciation."

"Appreciation for what?"

"For not letting me scare you off at that board meeting."

Maura frowned. "Were you trying to scare me off?"

Oren glanced down at his shoes. "I wanted to make sure you were serious about coming back here and making something of the theatre. And I didn't want to see Pastor Nick get hurt again." He took a deep breath, the internal struggle clear on his face. "I guess I need to apologize for that too. I never thought about your side of the story. But seeing you now, how you've embraced the town and become part of it, I figure something pretty serious must have happened to run you off the first time."

Maura nodded, unable to speak.

"Whatever happened, that's between you and God. And Pastor Nick, of course. For what it's worth, I think you're working out fine here."

"It's worth a lot." Maura drew him into an impulsive hug. Stiff and motionless at first, he finally gave her an awkward pat on the back.

"We don't have to get all mushy like this every time I come to class, do we?" he asked, pulling away.

Maura laughed. Now *that's* the Oren she knew. "Only if it's part of a scene. And speaking of scenes, how would you like to do us a huge favor and join our Christmas pageant?"

"I thought all the parts were already cast."

"They are, but Stu Pierson got called out of town this morning for a family matter. He was supposed to play the innkeeper in one of the skits, but he might not be back in time. I didn't know how I'd ever replace him so close to the performance, but now here you are, an answer to prayer. I'd be so thankful if you would step in."

Oren's chest puffed out a bit. Clearly, it pleased him to be considered an answer to someone's prayer. "When's rehearsal?"

16

There's a saying in the theatre that the worse the dress rehearsal is, the better the actual performance will be. Maura certainly hoped it was true because that meant the Christmas Gala should be worthy of a Tony Award.

A moving pack of bodies crammed the backstage area of the Music Box Theatre. And every one of them seemed to have some kind of problem that only Maura could solve.

"Ms. Sullivan, I can't find my costume."

"Mrs. Nelson's in charge of costumes. Go check with her, sweetie." Maura pointed the anxious fifth-grade girl toward Rachel, who stood by a clothing rack, handing out garments faster than a sales clerk at a clearance sale.

Maura turned her attention back to her clipboard but felt a tugging on her pant leg. She looked down to see five-year-old Timmy Reyes, decked out in shepherd garb, gazing wide-eyed up at her. "Yes, Timmy?"

"I forgot what I'm thupothe to thay."

She bit her lip to keep from smiling at Timmy's adorable lisp. "When your class finishes singing 'Away in a Manger,' you say, 'Jesus Christ is born.' Got it?"

Timmy pursed his lips and mouthed the words. He nodded his head sharply and shuffled away to join a bunch of pint-size shepherds.

Maura smiled and looked back at her checklist. Once everyone was in costume, she needed to go over the performance order and make sure each group knew their cues. Then—

A blood curdling shriek brought backstage activity to a halt. Everyone stood rooted in place until another scream spurred them to action.

"The bathroom!' Maura called out as she ran down the hall, closely followed by the entire cast and crew. They came to a stop outside the door to the women's restroom. Becca Nelson stood there, her back flat against the wall, her face white as a snowdrift.

Maura put her hand gently on the teenager's shoulder. "Becca, are you okay? What's wrong?"

"There's something in there."

Maura looked around. "Where?"

Becca lifted one arm straight out from her side and pointed at the closed door. "There."

This was overly dramatic, even for a member of the drama team. Resisting the urge to roll her eyes, Maura rubbed her hand up and down the girl's arm. "What did you see?"

"An animal."

An animal in the bathroom. *Rats.* Oh, she hoped not. She did not need to contend with a vermin infestation right now. But before she could do anything, she had to calm Becca down. Maura sighed with relief when she saw that Rachel had made her way through the curious crowd.

"Did you see a spider, Baby Doll?" Rachel slid her arm around her daughter, prying her off the wall.

The endearment, and the snickers it drew from some of the teens standing nearby, snapped Becca out of her panicked state. "*Mom*, please. No, I didn't see a spider. I saw a big, hairy animal."

"What kind of an animal?" Rachel asked.

Becca's head flopped from one side to the other. "I don't know. I went in to check my makeup and I saw this . . . thing in one of the stalls. I didn't stick around long enough to find out what it was."

Nick made his way through the crowded hallway. He came up beside Maura, putting a hand on her shoulder. "Would you like me to check it out?"

"Yes. Please." Relief shot through her. She'd been ready to wage war with whatever had taken over the bathroom, but she'd so much rather have Nick do it.

He squared his shoulders and winked. "If I'm not back in twenty minutes, send in reinforcements." He pushed open the door and went in.

The door closed automatically behind him, but not before an alarming odor hit Maura in the face. She wrinkled her nose in distaste. *Whew*, the mystery critter was mighty pungent.

"What the—"

Nick's exclamation penetrated the closed door. Then came the sound of a scuffle, some grunts from Nick, and the clatter of hard-sole shoes clacking on the tile. Maura and Rachel exchanged looks.

"Do you think we should help him?" Rachel asked.

Maura shook her head firmly. "Let's give him another minute." If Nick couldn't handle the situation, what chance did she have?

Silence. Not a sound came from within the bathroom. Maura leaned closer, her ear almost against the door, when it flew open. She jumped back, and a red-faced Nick rushed out, pulling the door shut behind him.

"It's a sheep," he said.

"A *what*?" Maura's disbelief was echoed by the adults standing in the hallway.

"A sheep. A big, woolly, white sheep."

Becca looked as if she might pass out. Rachel started laughing. And the kids in the hallway pushed forward, clamoring to get a look. As if they'd never seen a sheep before.

Maura still couldn't quite comprehend what Nick was telling her. "A sheep? How did a sheep get in my bathroom?"

"I brought it." A female voice called out of the crowd, and Samantha Pruitt made her way forward. Sam had only recently joined the youth group, but she'd struck Maura as a nice, down-to-earth girl. Definitely not the kind to pull this sort of prank.

"Why?" Maura asked.

"It was supposed to be a surprise, but that got ruined thanks to fraidy-cat here." She crooked her thumb at Becca. "You know when we're singing "The First Noel" and Billy Tyler carries in that stuffed sheep? It looks so lame. I thought it'd be cool to have a real sheep."

"But Billy's only six years old," Nick spoke up. "That animal must weigh at least forty pounds. There's no way he could carry it."

Sam hung her thumbs in the belt loops of her jeans and cocked her head to the side. "I know. But he could lead it in. Oscar's leash trained."

Maura felt like she'd stepped into an alternate universe. "The sheep's name is Oscar?"

"Yep. I raised him for a 4-H project, so now he's my pet." She turned a glare toward Becca. "He wouldn't hurt anybody."

Becca stuck out her tongue at Sam, who responded by making the universal symbol for "loser" with her fingers on her forehead. Maura snapped out of her shock. She had to put an end to this before she lost control of the whole night.

"Okay, you two, that's enough. Sam," she put her hand on the girl's shoulder, "I appreciate that you wanted to improve the Gala. But we've got enough to coordinate without bringing live animals into the mix. As soon as the dress rehearsal is over, I need you to take Oscar home. And keep him there. Okay?"

"All right," Sam agreed reluctantly. "But I still think he would have looked better than that stuffed thing."

Maura smiled and turned to the rest of the cast and crew. "For tonight, this bathroom is off-limits. Now let's get back on stage. We need to run through the whole show at least once tonight."

As the hallway cleared, Nick moved behind Maura and slipped his arm around her waist. "I'll say this, life with you is never boring."

Maura laughed. "Thanks." She turned in his grasp so that his arm was now around her back. With a smile she said, "You know you can't hold me this way."

"Sorry." He jumped back, looking embarrassed. "I get it. It's not appropriate around the kids."

"No, it's not that." She started down the hall and grinned over her shoulder at him. "You smell like Oscar."

The Gala Performance wasn't without its bumps. Timmy Reyes did forget his line, but he improvised by shouting out "Happy Birthday, Jesus!" so no one in the audience noticed. And not even Maura knew that one of the wise men misplaced the prop bottle that was supposed to be myrrh. She only discovered it after the show when she found Rachel's solution: a two-liter Pepsi bottle wrapped in gold foil. But those were minor glitches. Without a doubt, the gala was a huge success.

Maura climbed the front steps to the parsonage, happy but exhausted. It had been a long night. She'd stayed until she thanked the last parent and shook the last hand. Now she wanted nothing more than to fall into bed and sleep for a week.

She reached for the doorknob, but her hand stopped in midair when she saw a large note taped to the door. "Don't come in without knocking." What? Nick had left right after the gala concluded. She assumed he needed to put the finishing touches on his sermon for the next morning.

She knocked on the door three times and called out, "Hello!"

"Hold on." She heard Nick's voice from behind the door. Then footsteps. The door opened just a crack, and Nick pressed his face against it. All she could see was one eye, his nose, and the corner of his mouth.

"Shut your eyes."

"Excuse me?"

"Shut your eyes," he repeated. "I've got a surprise for you."

Her mild irritation at being kept outside fled, shooed away by a zing of anticipation. She closed her eyes and raised her chin. "Okay."

The door creaked open. Nick took both her hands and pulled her toward him. "Step up. Okay, now walk forward."

She heard the door shut behind them as they moved farther into the house.

"Good. Now, stop." Nick moved behind her, one hand on each shoulder. His breath was warm against her cheek as he whispered in her ear. "Open your eyes."

She opened her eyes but immediately closed and opened them again. She had to be sure she wasn't imagining this.

In the corner of the living room, across from the old brown couch, stood a Christmas tree. The twinkling lights weren't quite even, leaving bare spots here and there. The star at the top hung crooked, and it had no ornaments.

"Say something." Nick stepped beside her.

"I . . . I don't know what to say."

He sighed and dropped his chin to his chest. "I know it doesn't look like much, but—"

She grabbed his arm. "No. Don't apologize. It's wonderful." She'd never seen a more beautiful tree.

Nick looked up at her, one corner of his mouth lifting in a shy smile. "You like it?"

"I love it." Maura sniffed and wiped at the corner of one eye. "When did you have time?"

"While you were at the theatre today. Chris and some of the other men gave me a hand."

Maura smiled. That explained the placement of the lights. "Are there any ornaments?"

"Yes and no. Some of the ladies caught wind of what I was doing and tried to donate about a dozen boxes." He paused, looked at the tree, then looked back at her. "But I know how you feel about hand-me-downs. So I politely told them thank you, but we'd be picking out new decorations. Together."

"Really?"

"Really. Is that okay?"

She could only nod. Her nose tingled as tears welled in her eyes. But for once, they were happy tears.

———

"Good morning."

Maura looked over her shoulder, her hot mitt-clad hand still holding the handle of the open oven door. "You're up early. Did I wake you?"

He shook his head. "I woke up on my own and couldn't go back to sleep."

"Me neither." She closed the door and pushed a few buttons on the oven timer. "I thought only little kids did this on Christmas Day."

He put his hands in the front pockets of his jeans, his shoulders slightly hunched. "You know, I've kind of got that little kid feeling. Just think, we're completely free today. No appointments, no business meetings, no church events. Just a whole day with nothing on the calendar."

That was a big reason for her excitement, as well. The last few days had been non-stop. Between the successful Christmas Gala performance, ornament shopping with Nick, daily operations at the theatre, and all the special services at church, it seemed she was always rushing to the next event. It had been fun, but exhausting. "I've been meaning to ask how you managed to *not* have a church service on Christmas morning."

"That miracle was accomplished before I got here." He took a mug from the cupboard and headed for the pot of fresh coffee. "From what I'm told, about twenty years ago there was a huge storm on Christmas Day. Nobody could get out of their homes. Folks had no choice but to spend the day with their families. Pastor Wesson heard from so many people how it was the best Christmas they ever had, so he decided to make it a tradition."

"Here's to Pastor Wesson." She picked up her own coffee mug from the counter, raising it high. "I think it's wonderful, not only for families, but for all the church workers who deserve a real day of rest."

Nick started to raise his mug as well, but he stopped. He stood motionless, his eyes riveted to her as she took a drink of her coffee before she sat the cup down. He put his cup down, too, and walked over to her.

Without a word he reached out and took her left hand. He rubbed his thumb over the small diamond ring on her finger, and Maura let herself drift away on a wave of memories. They were back at the beach, the surf cheering them on and the warm breeze weaving around them like dancers at a maypole. It didn't matter that a crunchy white layer of frost coated everything on the other side of the kitchen window. At the moment, she was reliving one of the best days of her life.

"You're wearing your engagement ring." Nick's softly spoken words ended her daydream.

She hadn't worn either of her rings since the day she left Granger. When she moved back in with her father, she buried them at the back of a drawer under a pile of sweaters she had little cause to wear. She hadn't even looked at them until the day she packed up to move back to Granger. But the longer she'd been back and the better acquainted she'd become with her husband, the more often she'd taken the rings out and stared at them, remembering their promises. This morning seemed like the right time to slip one of them on.

Maura blinked hard a few times. "Merry Christmas."

Fingers entwined, Nick lifted her hand to his lips. "This is the best gift you could give me." He hesitated, a question settling in his eyes. "But you're only wearing the engagement ring. What exactly does that mean?"

Good question. It had taken Maura a while to figure out herself. "It means I'm committed to repairing our relationship. I want to be your wife again. But—"

Nick's brow furrowed. "I hate *buts.*"

"I know," Maura said with a laugh, "*but,* here it is . . . We promised the church council that until the end of six months, we'd live together platonically, like roommates."

He pulled her hand to his chest. "I never had a roommate like you." The low growl of his words vibrated beneath her palm.

She wanted nothing more than to throw reason and caution out the window. But at the same time, she was terrified of messing this up. "That's my point. We made a promise to the council, and I've got a lot of teenagers watching what I do. I don't want to give them the wrong impression, either."

"What impression is that? The one about it being good for a husband and wife to be together?"

She tried not to let the sarcastic bite of his statement phase her. "No," she went on calmly, "the impression that sex fixes broken relationships."

His eyes grew wide, and he took a step backward. "That was blunt. So what are you saying?"

"The six months will be up at the end of January. At that point, I think it would be best if I moved out of here and into the apartment over the theatre."

Nick dropped her hand. "Exactly how does that move us forward?"

"Once we're not living together, we can officially date and hopefully it won't be long before I can put on the other half of this ring set."

Maura knew her proposal didn't make any sense to Nick. It barely made sense to her. She was already in the house, after all. If everything went the way she hoped, she'd be moving out and moving back in within a month or so. But in her heart, she knew it was the right decision. Now if only Nick would see it her way.

If only Nick would say something.

"You're not counting, are you?"

Her question pulled a laugh out of him. Slowly, he shook his head. "No, I'm not. Just thinking. I hate to admit it, but you're right. This is a weird situation all the way around, isn't it?" He stepped forward, but stopped abruptly. "Can I still hug you?"

"Please." Maura smiled and walked up to him, arms open. His arms wrapped around her, pulling her close. It felt good to be held by him.

He looked over her head toward the oven. "What are you cooking?"

"A Christmas casserole."

Nick leaned back, his brows raised. "A casserole? I thought you hated casseroles."

"Think of it as a Christmas miracle. Besides, it's a recipe I got from Rachel, and there's not a noodle in it. It's eggs, onion, mushrooms, cheese . . . it's more like a big baked omelet."

"I see. Well, while we're waiting for it to finish baking, I've got something for you."

He took Maura's hand and pulled her into the living room to the Christmas tree.

"Have a seat." He motioned at the couch and knelt down, reaching beneath the tree. "Merry Christmas."

He handed her a large box wrapped in bright green paper and sporting a big red bow. From the abundance of tape, she could tell Nick had wrapped it himself, making it all the more special. She held it for a while, relishing her first Christmas present from him.

When she couldn't wait any longer, she tugged off the bow and ripped the paper away, uncovering a brown packing box. Pulling open the box flaps, she was greeted by the sight of Styrofoam packing peanuts and bubble wrap. She tried not to make a mess, but the peanuts overflowed the sides and spilled on the floor around her as she pulled a carefully wrapped object from the box.

Her breath caught in her chest. Nick, still kneeling on the floor, grinned like a little boy who had just caught a frog. She removed a piece of tape and slowly unwound the bubble wrap, revealing the amazing gift. The dainty teacup she held in her hand was a perfect match: white porcelain with delicate ivy leaves and vines curving and curling around the rim. It was her mother's china pattern. An exact duplicate of the cup Nick had accidentally broken so many years before.

"How did you ever find this?"

"It wasn't easy. I called the manufacturer and found out they don't make that pattern anymore. Thank God for eBay."

This time, Maura didn't even try to hold back the tears. They ran down her face, unabashed and unchecked. Nick took the cup from her hand and placed it safely on an end table. He got up from the floor and sat on the couch beside her, drawing her to him.

"I know I've hurt you, Maura." His voice was low and gentle in her ear as he rocked her, stroking her hair. "I put everybody else in front of you, and I drove you away."

The tears flowed harder now as thoughts assaulted her mind. *It's not all your fault. I haven't told you everything. You still don't know the whole truth.*

She had to tell him. They could only start a new life together if they built it on honesty and trust. No good could come from keeping secrets. But at the same time, telling him wouldn't change anything. It could never bring back what they'd lost. It could only serve to drive a wedge between them.

The truth hit her like a chandelier falling from the ceiling. The reason she ran, why she left without telling him the truth, wasn't only because of her anger toward Nick. She ran because of her own failings. Her own mistakes. And her fear that if Nick found out what had really happened, he'd leave her first.

She clung to Nick, pushing the thoughts aside, not ready to deal with reality. She couldn't tell him. Not now. They needed a fresh start, not another trip into the past. Sniffling, she pulled away, swiping the back of her hand across her eyes.

Nick took a handkerchief from his pocket and gently wiped the remaining tears from her face. "Can you forgive me?"

The simple act of service almost undid her again. But she smiled and answered, "I already have."

He drew her back to him, and she let herself settle into the shelter of his arms. Yes, she had forgiven Nick. Now she needed to find a way to forgive herself.

17

And one last signature here."

Wendell Crowley pushed another piece of paper in front of Maura. She lost track of how many times she'd signed her name, but with this, the last of a seemingly unending stack of forms, Maura officially became the legal owner of the Music Box Theatre, ending the current chapter of her life.

"Very good." Wendell picked up the document and added it to the stack on the side of his desk. "Pastor, if you'd be so kind, I need your signature here, and then we're done."

Excitement built within Maura as she watched Nick sign his one and only form. Just a little over seven months ago she'd sat in this room, thoroughly uncomfortable and wanting nothing more than to leave and get away from Nick. Today, she again itched to leave, but for a totally different reason.

Wendell handed Nick a check, grinning widely. "Congratulations to both of you on your inheritance. I'm sure Miss Hattie is looking down and smiling today."

Maura held a bulging manila folder containing the deed to the theatre and copies of all the papers she'd just signed. She had what she'd worked so hard for, and Nick had his donation for the church. Obviously, Miss Hattie had wanted to see the two of them together again, and Maura thought the woman would be happy to know she was close to getting what she wanted too.

"It's a good day for all of us," Nick said.

"Yes, it is." Wendell clasped his hands together in front of his chest, rocking forward on the balls of his feet. "What are your plans now, if you don't mind me asking?"

Maura hesitated. She knew what he wanted to hear; that she and Nick were living happily ever after. She hated to disappoint Wendell, but she didn't want to mislead him, either. "I'm moving out of the parsonage and into the apartment above the theatre."

The frown that took over the lawyer's face was so severe Maura feared he might be in pain. "Move out? But I thought it's been going well between you."

"It has," Nick said. "We're doing great. But we made some promises when Maura moved into the parsonage, and we need to keep them."

"And we need some space while we work out the rest of our issues. But look, we're engaged." She felt silly calling it that, but didn't know how else to describe their situation.

Maura wiggled her ring finger in front of Wendell and his smile rushed back.

"Fine, fine. One step at a time." He ushered them out of his office. "Remember, I'm only a phone call away if you need anything. Now go enjoy your day." He shut the door behind them.

Maura pushed the *down* button on the elevator, trying not to laugh.

"Engaged?" Nick asked. "How can we be engaged when we're already married?"

"I don't know." A giggle bubbled from her lips. "How could we live together when we were separated? Face it, you're in the middle of one crazy, mixed-up relationship."

"I'll say." He kissed her on the forehead just as the elevator doors slid open. Shaking his head, he stepped inside the car. "It's a good thing I love you, woman."

Maura hugged herself, pressing the folder against her chest. Yes, it was a good thing he loved her. Because now she knew she'd never stopped loving him.

"Tell me again why we're doing this?"

Maura ran smack into Rachel who had stopped in the middle of the stairway to ask her question. Shifting the box in her arms, Maura blew out a burst of air to move the bangs drooping over her left eye.

"I'll be happy to answer all your questions, *again*, but only after we get these boxes into the apartment."

Rachel frowned but continued up the steps, muttering something about how she wished they'd thought to fit an elevator into the renovation budget.

Despite the fact that her leg muscles protested the many trips up and down the stairs, and her best friend thought she was nuts, happiness surged through Maura like an electric current. She and Nick were creating a strong foundation on which to build their relationship. And now that she was out of the parsonage and in her own place, they could move on to the next phase.

Once inside the apartment, the two women set their loads down and sighed almost simultaneously. Turning to Maura, Rachel put her hands on her hips. "So?"

So. Maura looked around. Eclectic furnishings filled the room along with boxes she needed to unpack. The pale yellow walls were perfectly complemented by the red, yellow, and blue plaid couch in the living room area. Paintings of seascapes adorned the walls, reminiscent of the beaches of her childhood. Some of the items were new, some she'd bought second-hand, but she had chosen each piece with care. This was her new home. Even though she missed the idea of being around Nick as much, the thought still excited her. Finally, she had a place in Granger that was all her own.

Collapsing into a dark red, overstuffed chair, she motioned for Rachel to sit. "I don't think there's anything I can add to what I've already said. You know why I had to move out of Nick's place."

"I know why you *think* you had to move out, but I still don't agree with you." Rachel pushed off her tennis shoes with her toes and curled her stocking feet up under her on the couch.

Maura laid her head against the back of the chair. "Objection noted. Which makes it even nicer that you helped me out today. Thank you."

Rachel waved the compliment away. "I'm always saying I need to get more aerobic exercise. You just saved me the trouble of taking up jogging. But don't think you're going to distract me. Are you and Nick getting back together or not?"

Leave it to Rachel to forgo any bush beating. There was no point in trying to dodge the subject any longer. "That's the plan."

"So what's the point of moving you out just to move you back in again later? Although I must admit, this place is a lot homier than the parsonage." Rachel looked around the room. "It's got your touch all over it."

Maura smiled. Despite all the time they spent at the theatre, Rachel hadn't been in the upstairs apartment before. Maura had purposely done most of the work herself. The only other people who'd been there were the men who installed the new carpet and kitchen tile. Now, sitting here with her first official guest, satisfaction draped itself around Maura. The look of the place, the feel, was exactly what she wanted.

"In fact," Rachel continued, "I can't imagine you wanting to move out of here and back into the parsonage."

"That would have been true before. But I've come to realize the house isn't nearly as important as who's in it." Maura believed what she said. Still, there was a piece of her that wished she and Nick could live together here, in her brand new apartment. It was about the same size as the parsonage, and since it wasn't right next to the church, people would be less likely to drop by unexpectedly. But if Nick hadn't wanted to offend the congregation by redecorating, he surely wouldn't want to risk moving out altogether. And that was okay with her. She'd gotten used to the parsonage. Even the hideous tavern picture in the living room had grown on her.

Now she just had to convince Rachel that she wasn't crazy.

"Trust me. It makes sense to do it this way."

"You're sure?" Rachel pressed.

"Positive."

"Okay," Rachel nodded. "That's the last you'll hear from me on the subject. Just promise me one thing."

"What's that?"

"When it's time for you to move back in with Nick, you'll hire professional movers."

Maura leaned forward, joining her friend in a high-five. "Done."

Pulsating water beat down on Maura's back, easing the muscles in her shoulders. The last few weeks in her apartment had been wonderful. Between work, church, and dates with Nick, her days were full. It was such a treat to have a place to come home to at night and completely relax. The only drawback was lugging groceries up the stairs. Judging from her aching muscles, she'd done a little too much shopping the day before.

Turning toward the stream of water to wash her face, Maura caught sight of the plastic breast self-exam reminder hanging from the showerhead. She usually did her self-exam on the first of the month, but she'd been so busy she'd forgotten, promising each day to do it tomorrow. Frowning, she realized that tomorrow had come and gone almost two weeks ago.

"Get it over with now," she muttered.

She raised her left arm over her head and began manipulating her breast tissue with her right hand. As she did so, her mind wandered, ticking off all the items on her to-do list. Granger Community Hospital had booked a cardiac care seminar at the theatre the day before Valentine's Day. She had to remember to check with Rachel and make sure any artery-clogging snacks were removed from the candy counter and stowed out of sight during the event. And there was the youth group . . .

She lowered her left arm, raising her right and repeated the procedure in reverse.

The youth group had grown to the point where Lainie wanted to refurbish their room at church. It would be nice not only to paint, but to put in some high-tech audiovisual equipment and comfortable places for the kids to lounge. And maybe a snack machine. It seemed there was no way to get them to stop eating in the room, so the group might as well make a little money off it. And then . . .

Maura stopped short, pulled abruptly out of her thoughts and back to the present. She'd done a breast self-exam every month since she turned twenty-five. She knew the feel and texture of every inch of herself. But today, something was different.

Something was wrong.

Slowly, she moved her hand backwards. Her fingertips gently kneaded her skin, feeling the tissue beneath. There it was. It was small, but she felt it.

A lump.

She took a deep breath, but the room felt completely devoid of oxygen. She reached behind her, fumbling until she found the lever to turn off the water. Putting a hand against the tile wall, she steadied herself, forcing herself to breathe normally.

Be calm. Be calm.

Repeating the phrase over and over, she pushed the curtain aside, grabbed a towel and stepped out of the shower. She dried off, combed her hair, and got dressed, concentrating on each normal activity, putting off thinking about what she'd just found.

Sitting on the edge of the bed, she looked at the pictures on her nightstand. She and Nick on their wedding day. *Nick, I wish you were with me now.* Her mother and father on their wedding day.

Mom.

Be calm. Be calm.

Her mother had made her promise to take care of herself. "When you're old enough, do the breast exams and have your mammograms done. If they find it early, it's treatable." But her mother's cancer hadn't been found early. And Maura had watched it kill her.

She couldn't be calm. She couldn't will herself to hold it together. She couldn't do this on her own.

Lord, help me. Lord, help me.

Maura felt the panic subsiding. What had she read? Eight out of ten lumps end up being benign. Early detection is the key. These were good things to hold on to. She couldn't just sit there any longer. She had to do something.

She reached for the phone to call Nick's cell. She stopped in mid-dial, pushing the end button and breaking the connection. They'd had a wonderful, quiet dinner together the night before, talking about everything, including their schedules. He had meetings all morning. It wouldn't do any good to call him now.

Opening a small drawer in her nightstand she pulled out an address book. Tears stung Maura's eyes as she stared down at the name on the page. Painful memories assaulted her, drawing her back to another time, another phone call.

With shaking fingers, she dialed the number for Dr. Harris, her old OB/GYN.

18

Dr. Harris stepped back from the examining room table. "You can sit up, Maura."

The paper beneath her crackled as she sat up and swung her legs over the side. Pulling the sides of the flimsy gown together in front of her, Maura watched the doctor scribbling on her chart.

After what seemed like an eternity, Dr. Harris put the folder down and turned back to Maura. "You were right to come in. There is a lump. But I don't want you to panic." The doctor hurried on, her voice calm and reassuring. "The lump you found is extremely small. It could be nothing more than a cyst. But we do have to take it seriously."

Maura tried to smile, but her mouth wouldn't cooperate. Instead, she merely nodded.

Dr. Harris patted her on the shoulder. "Why don't you get dressed, and we'll talk about what happens next."

The doctor left the room and closed the door behind her. Maura didn't move. Instead, she thought about how she hated doctors' offices and hospitals.

Maura slid off the table and reached for her clothes. Poor Dr. Harris. She was a sweet person. In her late fifties, the woman had the demeanor of a favorite aunt, the kind who always has candy in her purse. But she'd been present at the worst moment in Maura's life, and Maura had never wanted to see her again. Yet here she was.

A few moments later she sat on a couch in the doctor's office. Sitting in a chair beside her, Dr. Harris explained the tests ahead of Maura.

"We should have the results of the mammogram and sonogram back in a week."

Maura took in a deep breath. In a week, she'd know one way or the other. She could do this.

"Thank you, Dr. Harris. That helps."

The doctor smiled and her eyes crinkled at the corners beneath her blue-rimmed glasses. "I'm glad. But I can't emphasize enough how important a support system is at a time like this. You need someone to be with you when you go for the tests and while you wait for the results. You are in for a very stressful time."

Maura bit down on her lower lip. Rachel would drop everything if she asked. But Rachel had her own family to worry about. And she needed to run the theatre while Maura had the tests done. That left only one other person who Maura could ask to take on such a responsibility.

As if reading her mind, Dr. Harris sat forward, her hands clasped in front of her. "You need to talk to your husband."

Maura opened her mouth to speak, but quickly clamped her lips shut. What was there to say? In the last few months, she and Nick had made huge strides towards mending their relationship. But now, in a time of crisis, all her old fears rushed back. Could she trust him to be there for her? When it came right down to it, Maura still didn't know if she could depend on him during a crisis.

Dr. Harris looked Maura in the eye. "I never told Pastor Shepherd about what happened. I honored your decision to keep it to yourself because telling him wouldn't change anything. But this time it can." Softening a bit, she patted Maura's hand. "I've heard through the Granger grapevine that you two are working toward reconciliation. That's good. You need to tell him what's happening with you. Trust me. You need his support now more than ever."

The rest of the meeting was a blur. Maura collected her papers and appointment slips and left the doctor's office with the woman's advice still ringing in her ears.

It was a fifteen-minute drive from the medical building to Faith Community Church, but to Maura, it could have been an hour. She hit every red light and got stuck behind every slow-moving car and farm truck on the road. As she inched along, she told herself there was no reason to worry. The lump was probably nothing, but even if it was something, she'd caught it early and it could be treated. But what if she had cancer? What would treatment mean?

Images of her mother flickered in her head like scenes on a movie screen. She saw the strong, vibrant woman who raised her, who sang while she worked in the garden and danced spur-of-the-moment jigs with Da. After the cancer diagnosis, all that changed. Maura watched her mother grow increasingly weaker. The chemo and radiation took its toll. The smell of the Irish food she used to love preparing for her husband, like his favorite corned beef, now made her sick. She lost weight, and she lost her hair. She lost her energy and her interest in doing anything other than lie in bed as the television droned on. She would smile weakly whenever Maura came into her room to sit on the bed beside her, but she didn't have the strength to carry on a conversation. In Maura's strongest memory, she held her mother's bony hand while Vanna White turned letters on *Wheel of Fortune*. Mom had died the next week.

Behind her, a horn blared. The light had turned green. Jerking her foot from the brake pedal she stomped on the gas, making the car lurch forward through the intersection.

Is that what she had to look forward to? Losing everything that meant anything to her until one day she couldn't even respond to the people who loved her? And what about Nick? Her Da was a wonderful, loving father, but he'd never been the same after his wife died. If she did have cancer, would Nick go through the same thing?

By the time Maura pulled into the church parking lot, she was a wreck. Her hands held the steering wheel in a white-knuckled grip. It was as if she was back on that Ferris wheel, suspended in midair, not knowing when it would start up again or in which direction it would move.

But she couldn't fall apart now. She forced herself to take deep breaths. She should pray, she wanted to pray, but her mind was such a jumbled mess of emotions she couldn't put together a coherent thought.

"God, help me," she whispered. "God, help me."

Little by little, each tensed muscle in her body relaxed. She looked around the lot, hoping no one had noticed her erratic behavior. Thankfully, the only cars appeared to be those of the staff, parked near the office.

She reached for her purse in the passenger seat, taking a deep breath. *Help me keep it together, Lord.*

Walking to the office, Maura distracted herself by focusing on the sights around her. The paint on the corner of the building was peeling, as if someone had run into it with something big and bulky. A soda can lay under one of the bare bushes flanking the office wall. She hoped one of the teens hadn't left it there.

The teens. How would she tell them the news? And how would they take it if she—

Stop it!

Maura halted abruptly, shaking her head to drive out the tormenting thoughts. *Help me, Lord. Help me think good thoughts. Keep my focus on you.*

She grabbed the knob on the office door, slowly pushing it open, and stepped inside. Praise music played softly in the background, competing with the hum of a copy machine in an adjoining room. A large plate of cookies sat on the front desk, permeating the air with the smell of chocolate and vanilla. The sounds and smells wrapped around her, providing a moment of normalcy in the midst of her chaos.

Sitting behind the desk, Pauline Ramirez, the church secretary, looked up from her computer, a smile of recognition on her face. "Hi, Maura. Good to see you."

Maura forced a smile in return. "You too. Sorry to be blunt, but I really need to see Nick. Is anybody with him?"

Pauline's brow creased slightly. "No, he's alone. Are you okay?"

Maura nodded, fighting back the emotions that threatened to shatter her composure. "I just . . . can I go in?"

"Sure. I'll let him know you're here." Pauline waved her through, at the same time pushing the intercom button on the phone.

As Maura walked down the hall, she heard Pauline's voice behind her. "Pastor, Maura's here to see you. She's on her way in."

Nick's office door shot open before she reached the end of the hall. "This is the best surprise I've had all day."

He was so happy to see her, so open and available, it was like a knife to her heart. *Why now?* Why when they were just starting to put their lives back together did they have to face another crisis? Hadn't they been through enough?

Maura opened her mouth to speak, but no words came out. She felt her lips twist and contort, the corners pulling down into a frown as tears burned her eyes. The smile fell from Nick's face. He reached for her, and she rushed into his arms, letting go of all the sorrow and fear that had gripped her since that awful moment in the shower.

Holding her tightly, Nick led her into his office. He pulled her down next to him on the couch and rocked her.

"Be with Maura, Father." He murmured a soft prayer against her hair. "Whatever she's facing let her know she's not alone."

His voice was barely a whisper, but it gave her the strength to face what she had to do. Taking huge, gulping breaths, Maura pushed away from Nick. Her tears had left a big wet spot on the front of his shirt. "I'm . . . sor . . . sorry," she forced out.

Nick grabbed a box of Kleenex from the table beside the couch and handed it to her. "It'll dry, honey. What's wrong? Can you tell me?"

Nick waited while Maura blew her nose and wiped her eyes. She told him everything. How she found the lump in the shower, about her appointment with Dr. Harris, and the tests she needed to have over the next few days.

"I'm sorry to barge in and dump this on you. I know you're always so busy, but . . ." She wanted to ask him to be with her when she went for the tests. She wanted to know that he would be by her side through it all, even if the worst happened. But she was afraid. What if he let her down?

Nick took her hands in his, raising one to his lips. "You have nothing to apologize for. Now, the doctor told you it's probably nothing to be worried about, right?'

"Yes, but—"

"No *buts*. You know how I feel about those." He pushed her hair back from her face and laid his palm against her cheek. "We're holding on to hope unless we find out otherwise, and then we'll deal with it. Right now, let's take it one step at a time."

Kissing her on the forehead, he got up from the couch and walked over to his desk. He punched a button on the phone.

"Yes?" Pauline's voice came through the speaker.

"Pauline, would you and Pastor Chris come into my office, please? And bring my schedule with you."

Maura wrapped her arms around herself, trying to ward off the chill that enveloped her. This is how it would be. Not only was he going to show her his busy schedule, but he planned to pawn her off on the associate pastor. Why had she dared allow herself to think anything had changed? As always, the congregation came first.

The door opened. Pauline and Pastor Chris walked in, their faces a mixture of concern and confusion. Maura steeled herself for the inevitable. But Nick returned to his place beside her, putting a protective arm around her and pulling her close.

"I need to attend to an important family matter, so I'll be unavailable for at least a week, maybe more." Nick's voice was strong and steady. He gave Maura's shoulder a little squeeze as he continued. "Pauline, go over my calendar and reschedule whatever you can. Chris, I know I'm asking a lot, but if there's anything that can't be rescheduled, I'll need you to take care of it. That includes services on Sunday."

Maura gaped at Nick. "Are you sure? You never miss a service."

"We'll be there," Nick said with a nod. "I just won't be able to prepare the sermon. Pastor Chris is more than capable of taking over for a few Sundays."

The young pastor didn't hesitate. "Don't worry about a thing. What else can we do?"

"Pray," Nick said. "I'd rather not go into the details right now, but just pray. God will take care of the rest."

With assurances that they'd keep the couple in their prayers, Chris and Pauline left the room. Maura turned to Nick, smiling for the first time that day.

"You dropped everything for me. You didn't need to do that."

Nick threaded his fingers in her hair, his hand settling on the base of her neck. "Of course, I did. You're my wife, and I love you. We're going to get through this. Together."

With a sigh, Maura fell against his chest and let him hold her. *Together.* What a beautiful word that was.

19

At the sound of knocking on the door. Maura lifted her head from the book in her lap. "I'll get it," she called.

Maura's original plan had been to spend the week holed up with Nick, away from inquisitive well-wishers. But her friends had other ideas.

She'd had more visitors to her apartment over the last few days than in the entire month she'd lived there. Rachel, the only other person she'd told about finding the lump, had insisted Maura take some time off from the theatre until all her tests results were in. She stopped by daily to fill Maura in on business and, Maura was sure, to check up on her.

Lainie came by the day before. Although she didn't know the nature of the problem, she still had the youth group kids make a card for her. They took a big piece of poster board, folded it in half, and decorated it with pictures, signatures, and greetings. It now stood like a centerpiece in the middle of Maura's dining table.

Opening the front door, she gasped. Oren Thacker, the most unexpected visitor of all, stood on the landing, twisting his gloves nervously between his hands.

"Oren. Hi, won't you come in?"

He nodded, grunting out a hello of his own, and walked past her into the living room.

"Nick," she called toward the kitchen, "Oren's here."

While she and Oren had definitely made strides in their relationship, they never socialized outside of church or the theatre. To have him show up with no advance warning made her a little nervous. Had he heard about Nick staying in the apartment? She hoped he wasn't there to deliver another message from the church council about the importance of appearances.

Nick came out of the kitchen, wiping his hands on a dish towel. "Oren, good to see you." He grabbed Oren's extended hand, giving it a hearty shake. "I was just throwing together some lunch. Want to join us?"

"No, thank you. I'm glad you're here, though, because I came to speak to both of you."

Uh oh. This couldn't be good. Maura braced herself for the scolding to come. "Would you like to sit down?"

With another stiff nod, Oren dropped into the red chair. As Nick sat beside her on the couch, Maura took a deep breath and smiled. "What's up?"

Rather than answer Maura, he turned, speaking directly to Nick. "As you know, there was a church council meeting yesterday. You were missed."

Nick put a casual hand on Maura's knee. "It couldn't be helped."

"I know. Pastor Chris shared your situation."

"He *what?*" Nick's voice came out hard as granite.

"Not any details," Oren said in a rush. "Just that there's a family emergency and to pray. But with you staying here with Maura, it sets a mind to wondering."

I'll just bet it does. Maura put her hand on Nick's, squeezing his fingers. Glancing at him, she saw a little muscle tic working away in his jaw. He was probably counting too. She wanted to lash out, to tell Oren that the council had no business poking into their personal life, but she stopped herself. Over the past few months, she'd come to realize that, if she and Nick reconciled, certain aspects of her life would be open to scrutiny. She'd made her peace with it. As much as she hated to admit it, the personal life of the pastor was the council's business, to a point. She would get much farther talking to Oren, trying to understand why he felt the way he did, rather than brooding in silence.

"Oren," she began gently, "I know it must seem odd that Nick is staying in the apartment with me. But I assure you, he's here to give me emotional support, and that's all. He's been sleeping in the spare room, so it's really not any different from when I lived at the parsonage. I know you didn't like that arrangement, but—"

Oren held up his hands. "I think you misunderstood. I . . . the council . . . we don't have any objection to Pastor Nick staying here. You two are married, after all."

This was new. "Then what were you wondering about?" Maura asked.

He paused, taking a moment to smooth out his now mangled gloves on one knee. "Well, you haven't been around the theatre in a few days. Since you own it free and clear now, that got us to thinking you might have decided to sell it and move on." Oren frowned, and his voice became gruff. "We don't like the idea of you leaving Granger."

Maura smiled as a swell of emotion tingled her nose and eyes. "I think that's the sweetest thing I ever heard. I promise. I'm not planning to sell the theatre or move away."

"Well, that's good to hear." Oren reached into his jacket and pulled out a small envelope. "I asked Rachel Nelson what we could do to help out, and she said food would be good, so we got you a gift certificate to Gandino's."

Maura sent up a silent thank you to Rachel. The Italian restaurant was relatively new in town and had quickly become one of Maura's favorites. "Thank you so much."

"And, don't worry, we won't be sending over any casseroles," Oren added, almost as if he read her mind. "Rachel told us how you feel about them."

Maura bit her lip. She must seem like the most ungrateful woman on earth. "I wish she hadn't done that."

"Nonsense." He waved a hand in the air. "How's a body supposed to know what you like unless you tell them? I can't stand the things, myself, but some folks love them."

Oren rose to his feet, knees popping. "I'd best be on my way." He started for the door, causing Nick and Maura to jump up and follow him out. "We're praying for the two of you. If you need anything, make sure you let us know."

"Oren."

The man was at the top of the stairs when Maura called his name. He turned around, his look expectant.

"There is something you can do for me. Rachel's taken over so much, but I don't want to overload her. Can you run the Thursday night drama class?"

He stood up straighter, his chest puffed out so that for a moment he seemed in danger of toppling over. Putting a hand to the banister he smiled broadly, transforming his features. "I think I could do that. But we'll be expecting you back soon."

Standing behind Maura, Nick slipped his arms around her waist. They stayed that way as Oren made his way down the stairs and out the front door.

"I don't think I've ever seen him so happy." Nick's voice was warm in Maura's ear. "It was sweet of you to do that."

"I think Oren and I are finally starting to understand each other. But enough about him." She turned in Nick's arms, putting her hands on his shoulders. "Weren't you fixing lunch when he got here?"

"It's ready, but it's not going anywhere. Suddenly, I'm not so hungry anymore."

They came together in a reunion as sweet as the first time their lips had ever met. Maura's hands moved to his neck, into his hair, as she deepened the kiss, wanting to be as close to him as possible.

When they separated, both were breathing a little harder. Before he spoke, Maura read the unasked question burning in his eyes.

"I love you, Maura. I want to be your husband again, in every sense of the word. There's nothing stopping us now but each other."

He was right. It was clear now that the church council, and probably everyone in the town, recognized them as a married couple. A unique couple, granted, but still a married one. They were released from all the obligations and expectations that had held them back. But there was still one huge obstacle Nick wasn't seeing.

She caressed his cheek. "You have no idea how much I want to be with you, in the biblical sense. But if we do that now, there's a chance I could get pregnant."

Nick blinked. "That would be wonderful."

"Not now, it wouldn't." Maura saw his disappointment and rushed on. "Think about it. We still don't have my test results back. I know we're believing it's nothing, but what if the worst happens? What if I do have cancer? That could mean chemo, and the baby—"

Her breath caught in her chest. Chemo would kill a baby. She couldn't go through that kind of pain again.

Nick's face softened and he drew her back to him, cradling her head against his chest. "You're right. I didn't think it through that far. We'll wait, and I'll take cold showers."

Maura laughed and looked up at him. "Thanks for understanding. Now maybe we should get out of this hallway?"

With a nod, Nick released her. They walked back into the apartment just as the phone rang.

"Please be the doctor with good test results," Nick muttered behind her.

"Amen to that." Maura picked up the receiver. "Hello."

Nick raised his eyebrows in question. She mouthed, "It's the doctor," before giving her full attention to the woman on the other end of the phone. After jotting down some notes on a pad, she said thank you and hung up.

"Well?" Nick asked.

Maura let out the breath she'd been holding since she hung up. "Well, I hope you like your showers cold. The results from the mammogram and the sonogram were both inconclusive."

"Both? Isn't that unusual?"

"No. Not according to the doctor." Maura was weary. Tired of questions, tired of answers that answered nothing. Just talking now felt like a chore.

"What does that mean?"

She sat on the couch, elbows on knees, her hands clasped in front of her. "Now I need to have a biopsy. After that we'll know for sure one way or the other. It's scheduled for four o'clock tomorrow."

Nick knelt in front of her, placing his hands over hers. "Do you need to stay in the hospital overnight?"

"No." She shook her head. "It's an outpatient procedure. They stick a needle into the lump, pull out a sample, and some time next week we'll have the answer."

"More waiting."

Maura nodded. "You know, I thought I'd fall to pieces if I got any more bad news, but I'm kind of numb right now." She slid off the couch and onto the floor beside Nick.

He took her in his arms, pulling her onto his lap. "We'll get to the other side of this."

"I know." She pressed her face against his chest. "Will you pray with me?"

His arms tightened around her and together they sat on the floor and prayed. They thanked God for who He was and for the blessings He'd given them. They asked Him to be with them and to bring healing if that was His will. A gentle peace settled over Maura, replacing the tired numbness that claimed her body minutes earlier. What was that Scripture? *All things work together for good to them that love God.*

She was back with Nick, in his arms and being supported by him in a way she'd never thought possible. She was part of a community that cared about her. Her life was full and rich in ways she couldn't have dreamed. God had certainly done good for her already. Maura knew He wouldn't leave her now.

They sat in silence, comforting each other.

"Nick." Maura looked up at her husband.

"Yes?"

"Would you go on a date?"

Nick grinned. "That depends. What did you have in mind?"

"I thought we could get dressed up and go to Gandino's." She picked up the gift card and waggled it in the air. "My treat."

The date was a great idea. Instead of sitting around, wondering what else could possibly go wrong, Maura chose to celebrate life. And Nick intended to make it a celebration she wouldn't soon forget.

He insisted on returning to the parsonage to get ready. After putting on his best suit, he drove around in vain looking for fresh flowers. Finally, he went into Hilda's Gift Shop and Scrapbook Hut to find a suitable substitute.

Hilda herself walked out of the backroom to greet him. "My, my," she said with a whistle, "aren't you spiffy? You look like you're ready to preach a sermon, Pastor."

Nick chuckled. "Thank you. But I've got a date."

"A date?" Hilda's eyebrows shot up.

"With my wife. And I want to give her a little gift."

Hilda nearly melted in front of him. "How romantic. Well, you can't go wrong with these." She led him over to a shelf filled with red satin-covered boxes of chocolates. "The ladies love these."

Nick took the box she handed him. She grabbed his arm and pulled him across the store, talking as they went. "Oh, and if you really want to impress that wife of yours, you can get one of these too." Nick now found himself holding a white stuffed teddy bear as well as the candy.

"And—"

"Hilda!" He stopped her in midflight as she headed toward a display of enormous perfume bottles. "This will do just fine. Thank you."

Hilda beamed as she rang up his purchases. She was obviously quite pleased to be a part of the pastor's romantic endeavor.

By the time he arrived back at Maura's apartment, he felt a little foolish. Standing in front of the door, Nick looked down at the red candy box and the bear in his hands. What if he was making too big a deal out of this? Maura wanted to go out, sure, but what if she thought he was pushing too hard?

It was too late to turn back now.

Nick rapped his knuckles against the door. Maura opened it, and the sight of her made his mouth dry up. Her simple black dress emphasized all the physical features he loved, while the smile on her face reflected her inner beauty. She was, as they say, the whole package.

"Wow."

Her smile broadened. "I take it that means you approve." She pointed at the gifts in his hands. "Are those for me?"

He handed them to her. "I wanted to get you flowers, but everyone who sells them was out."

"These are very nice. Thank you."

She turned and Nick followed her into the apartment. "It's a beautiful evening," he said. He needed to fill the void with conversation, no matter how inane. "Still cold enough to see your breath, but no snow or rain, so the sidewalks are clear."

"That's good." Maura put the presents he'd brought on the dining table, right in front of the card from the youth group. She crossed her arms, cocking her head to the side. "Are you all right?"

"Me? I—" There was no reason to dance around the truth. He might as well confess. "Actually, I'm a little nervous."

"Why?" She sounded surprised.

"I'm still amazed that God brought us together again. Ever since you came back to Granger, I've realized how much I missed you and what a huge mistake I made by not going after you when you left."

She dropped her hands to her sides, rubbing the palms on her hips. "I was a lousy pastor's wife. I didn't help out with the congregation the way you wanted me to. I figured you didn't come after me because your life was easier without me in it."

Her words hit him like a fresh blow. Had he really made her think he saw her that way? As a hindrance to his ministry?

"Maura, no. I felt like my heart ripped in two when I found out you'd gone."

Pain swam in her eyes. "Then why didn't you come after me?"

Nick ran a hand through his hair. Was she serious? "Because you told me not to. You left me that note saying you'd gone and you didn't want to talk to me. You specifically told me not to come after you."

Her hand moved to her mouth, and he knew that beneath it, she was probably chewing on her lip. "I was so upset that day. I don't even remember writing the note."

"Trust me. You did. But I couldn't just let you leave. I had to do something, so I called your father."

Her hand fell from her face and her skin paled by a shade. "You what?"

"I called your father. He said I'd hurt you more than I'd ever know. That you refused to speak to me, and our marriage was over for good. He said that if I loved you as much as I said I did, I'd never call again." Nick paused. "He never told you, did he?"

Silently, she shook her head. Nick wanted to be angry with Joe Sullivan, but he couldn't. The man was protecting his daughter. How could Nick fault him for that?

He reached out, taking both of Maura's hands in his. "I'm sure your father did what he thought was best for you. Did you tell him what happened between us?"

She nodded, but still remained quiet. So Nick went on. "If we're going to start over, don't you think it's time you told me why you decided to leave that day?'

Maura stiffened, almost jerking her hands from his. "I do," she said, "and I will. But not tonight. For one thing, I've got makeup on, and if I start crying it'll run all over my face." Her attempt at humor fell flat, but she took a deep breath and forced a smile. "Right now, you need to know that I love you.

Having you with me through this means more than you can possibly imagine. I don't want to talk about biopsies or past sins or anything sad tonight. I just want us to go out and enjoy being together. Can we do that?"

Once again, she refused to tell him the whole truth. She said she loved him, but he couldn't wonder if part of her still didn't trust him. Was that the reason she kept holding back? Regardless, he couldn't push her, especially considering all she was dealing with.

"Of course. Light and carefree it is." Nick picked up her coat from the back of the easy chair and held it open for her. As she slid her arms into the satin lining, he circled his around her, pulling her close against him, and kissed the top of her head. He'd do as she asked, for now. But sooner or later, she needed to tell him everything. And the longer she waited, the more Nick dreaded what she might have to say.

20

I don't have cancer!"

Maura dropped the cordless phone receiver on the table, letting out a whoop as she ran to Nick. She threw her arms around his neck, and he lifted her up, spinning her around.

"Thank you, Lord," Nick shouted to the roof. When he set her down, he cradled her face in his hands and kissed her. "Now," he said, drawing back a little, "tell me everything the doctor said."

"It's not cancer. It's a cyst. Most likely it will go away on its own. Dr. Harris wants me to have another mammogram in six months, just to be safe, but she said there's nothing to worry about." It came out in a rush, as though all the pent-up anxiety of the last two weeks was contained in those words. Maura took a breath. "It's over."

"It's over," Nick repeated. "Now we can get on with our life together."

She laid her head on Nick's chest, holding him tight around the middle. How she wished they could start fresh, right at that moment. But something still stood between them. The secret she'd been keeping all these years reared up, staring her in the face, daring her to push it into a dark corner as she always did.

Well-worn justifications replayed in her head. They'd been through so much already, couldn't she just ignore it? What good would it do to expose such an old, festering wound?

But this time, Maura knew she couldn't rationalize it away. She had to tell him the truth. It was the only way they could go forward.

"Nick, let's sit down." She took his hand and pulled him to the couch. "I need to tell you what happened the day I left."

Nick still held her hand, the pad of his thumb rubbing gently across her knuckles. She drank him in, memorizing the love in his eyes, hoping she'd still see it there after he heard what she had to say.

"I was sick, but it was much worse than you thought. I, well—" This was harder than she'd expected it to be.

"Actually, it started before that night. I'd been trying to tell you for weeks, but there was never a good time. I wanted it to be special, but you were always busy, or tired, or . . . something." She took a deep breath and blurted it out the way she should have done years ago. "I was pregnant."

His thumb stopped moving. "Pregnant?"

Maura swallowed hard, giving a quick nod of her head. "The day I called you, I wanted you to come home because I was sick. I had a miscarriage."

Nick jerked his hand from hers, reeling back as if she'd slapped him.

"I'm so sorry." She reached for him, but he jumped to his feet and moved across the room.

"I don't understand." He paced back and forth, one hand pinching the back of his neck. "Why didn't I know you were pregnant?"

"I didn't know myself until I was almost three months along."

"What? How could you not know?"

She'd asked herself the same question over and over again. "My periods have always been irregular, so I didn't think about that. And I was sick to my stomach all the time and losing weight, so I thought I just had the flu."

"Why didn't you tell me?"

Heat burned Maura's cheeks. "I tried. But you always had something going on. It was impossible to get any time alone with you."

"You should have made me listen."

"You're right, I should have. But just a week after I found out I was pregnant, I had the miscarriage, and it didn't matter anymore." All the emotions from that time flooded back. The joy, the pain, the fear that she'd done something to cause the loss of their baby. Maura choked it all down, determined not to fall apart.

"It didn't matter?" Nick's voice was raw, ragged. "How could you not tell me that our baby . . . that our baby—"

Maura watched her husband struggle to deal with the news, and her heart broke. Nick spent his life being strong for everyone else. She'd never seen him like this.

She got up, moving toward him, wanting to comfort him, to be strong for him. "Nick, I'm—"

"You're what?" He stopped her where she stood. "You're sorry?"

"Yes."

"You lied to me."

She wanted to protest. She hadn't lied, not really. But that would only make matters worse. A lie of omission was just as bad as a bald-faced lie. And she'd been carrying this one around for years.

Nick raked his hand through his hair, still pacing. "I know I did a lot of things wrong, but I never lied to you. I always thought we could trust each other to be honest, no matter what."

"Of course, you can trust me."

"We had a baby together, and you kept that from me. I never had the chance to celebrate that miracle, or to grieve its loss." His hands sliced through the air. "How can I trust you now?"

Panic grabbed Maura by the throat. He was talking as if they had no future. "Nick, I made a mistake. I made lots of mistakes. I shouldn't have waited so long to tell you I was pregnant. After the miscarriage, I didn't see what good it would do to tell you. It was over, and I didn't think I'd ever see you again. I thought I was sparing you the pain I'd gone through. But I was wrong. About all of it."

Nick finally stopped moving. He stood in front of her, stiff as an iron rod, eyes cold as steel. "I thought we'd be together forever. I didn't think anything you told me today would change that. Guess I was wrong too."

He turned on his heel and walked out, pulling the door shut forcefully behind him.

Maura stood there alone. Only the buzzing in her ears intruded on the room's silence. The joy at receiving a clean bill of health from the doctor had disappeared. The bright colors she'd chosen so carefully to make the apartment a cheerful place seemed to mock her now. Her soul felt cold, empty. Barren.

The outcome she'd feared most had happened. She'd been completely honest with Nick, and he'd left her.

She'd cried so much in the last few weeks, Maura didn't think she had any tears left. But now, as she put her face in her hands and wept, she realized that was one more thing she'd been wrong about.

An hour later, Maura sat at her dining table, staring blankly at the white stuffed bear perched in front of her. She'd called Nick's cell phone, but it had gone straight to voice mail. She hadn't tried again. Clearly, he didn't want to talk to her right now.

The knock on the door made her heart leap. He'd come back! She ran across the room, twisted the knob, and jerked the door open. But it wasn't Nick who stood on the other side.

"Rachel." She couldn't keep the disappointment out of her voice.

Rachel's smile turned into an instant frown. "Don't get so excited," she grumbled. "I just wanted to see how you're doing."

"I'm sorry. Come on in." She stepped aside and waved her friend into the room. "I'm glad you're here. This just hasn't been the best day."

Rachel whirled around, catching Maura by the shoulders. "Did your test results come in?"

Maura nodded. "Yes, but—"

"Honey, I'm so sorry." Rachel engulfed her in a hug. "But you're gonna get through this. I'll be here for you. Whatever you need, you just let me know."

"No, you don't understand." Maura wriggled out of her friend's grip. "The tests results were great. It's just a cyst. I'm fine. No cancer."

"I don't understand." Rachel's brows scrunched up. "Why aren't you celebrating? And why do you look like you just lost your best friend?"

"Because I did." Maura collapsed into the easy chair. "I told Nick today. About the baby."

Rachel drew in a quick breath. "Oh, boy." She sat on the couch, angling her body toward Maura. "I guess he didn't take it too well."

"Hardly. I think he's out of my life for good."

"You don't know that."

"You didn't see him, Rachel. He was so angry. And hurt. He said he could never trust me again." Maura pinched the bridge of her nose. "How can he ever forgive me?"

"Let me ask you, how long did it take you to get over losing the baby?"

Maura leaned her head against the back of the chair, eyes closed. After the miscarriage, she'd thought about the baby every day, the pain so intense it was almost physical. But with time, the ache dulled, until it became a traumatic, distant memory.

"I don't know exactly," she answered, "but it was a long time."

"Of course, it was. Now look at it from Nick's perspective. Not only did he just find out there was a baby, but he found out about the miscarriage and that you kept it from him. That's a lot to process all at once. I'm sure he's hurt and angry and a whole slew of other emotions all at the same time." Rachel leaned forward, her eyes intense. "But that doesn't mean he'll stay that way. Give him some time."

What Rachel said made sense, but Maura knew how easy it was to ignore a problem rather than face it. "What if time doesn't help? What if he won't talk to me again?"

Rachel smiled. "You know better than anyone how small this town is. The two of you will run into each other whether you want to or not. He won't be able to avoid you forever."

"I guess you're right." Maura sighed. "So what do I do now?"

"Now you live." Rachel slapped Maura on the knee. "You stared cancer down and beat it."

Maura rolled her eyes. "You're being a bit overly dramatic. I didn't beat it. It was never there to begin with."

"Still, the possibility of cancer was there, and you faced it. This is a time to celebrate."

Rachel was so positive, her tone so upbeat, Maura felt encouraged despite the fact that her relationship with Nick had just imploded. "What did you have in mind?"

"I'm taking you to lunch at Rosie's Diner. The cheesecake's to die for. Better yet, it's to live for. And we're both going to have a big piece for dessert."

Maura nodded. "Just give me a second." She stood up and headed to the bathroom. Rachel was right about Nick. He needed time to deal with everything she'd just told him. After the miscarriage, she believed their life as husband and wife was over. But God brought her back and gave her a second chance. But would He show her the same grace a second time?

⁓

Nick went straight from Maura's apartment to the one place he could always count on: the church. Years earlier, when he'd found himself single, abandoned by his wife, he'd sought refuge there, finding comfort in burying himself in the Lord's work. He expected to find the same solace now.

But it didn't quite work out that way.

When he got to the office, Pastor Chris was leaning on the desk beside Pauline, looking at something on her computer monitor. As Nick walked in the door, they both looked up, surprise evident on their faces.

"Pastor Nick," Pauline said, "we didn't expect to see you today."

Chris's expression was serious. "Is everything all right?"

Nick nodded. "The crisis is over. Everything's fine, and I'm back to work. If you two have a minute, we can go over the schedule and you can get me back up to speed."

Chris and Pauline exchanged looks, then followed Nick into his office. For the next thirty minutes, they filled him in on upcoming meetings and appointments. Nick penciled more and more things into his calendar until he'd filled in almost every day for the next month.

"Thanks, Pauline. If anything else comes up, let me know. Now I need to talk to Pastor Chris."

Pauline got up to leave, but stopped at the door. "It's good to have you back, Pastor."

After she'd gone, a somber Chris leaned forward in his chair. "Do you want to tell me what's going on?"

On the other side of the round table, Nick leaned back, his elbow on the armrest of his chair and his fingertips resting against his temple. No, he really didn't want to talk about his personal pain. He was in the business of helping others. As a leader, he needed to set an example, hold a higher standard. To admit to the disastrous state of his life was like admitting he'd failed at his work. Failed God.

"I don't know if I can," he said.

Chris picked up a pen and fiddled with the cap. "I care about what you're going through, as my pastor and as my friend. But if you're not ready to talk, I won't push you." Chris gathered his papers from the desk and stood up to leave.

In the year and a half that Chris had been with Faith Community, Nick had come to regard him not only as a gifted minister, but as a trusted friend. Chris was probably the only person in Granger he could talk to about personal issues.

"Wait," Nick called to him. "You're right. Let's sit on the couch. This could take a while."

Nick told him the whole story. About the cancer scare, his near reconciliation with Maura, and the devastating news about the miscarriage. As he talked, Nick felt the emotions roil up inside him again, like a soda can being shaken. What must

Chris think of him? Was he wondering how a man could be so wrapped up in his work that he didn't know about his wife's pregnancy? But Chris just listened, no evidence of judgment on his face.

"That's the whole story," Nick concluded. "She lied to me. And now our marriage is over. For good this time."

"Are you sure?" Chris asked, his voice soft. "It sounds like you both made mistakes, and she forgave you. Why can't you do the same?"

Nick chafed at the statement. As a pastor, he knew better than anyone the importance of forgiveness. "Well, of course, I'll forgive her. I don't have a choice, do I? But how can I forget what happened? I'm still grieving the death of a child I didn't even know existed until a few hours ago."

"Of course. When it comes right down to it, this is between you and God. Once you're right with Him, you'll know how to approach Maura." Chris leaned forward and grabbed Nick's hand. "Let's pray."

By the time Chris walked out of his office, Nick's mind had cleared. He still felt hurt and angry, but maybe in time, that would pass. For now, he needed to submerge himself in prayer, the Bible, and serving others. It had worked for him before and he was sure it would work again now.

His stomach rumbled, a reminder that lunch time had come and gone some time ago. Grabbing his coat, he went back to the outer office. "I'm walking over to Rosie's," he said to Pauline. "Will you call ahead and order me a roast beef sandwich to go? And order something for yourself if you'd like."

"That's okay. I already ate." Pauline shooed him out the door. "I'll call right now."

Once outside, frigid blasts of air assaulted him. He took a deep breath, feeling the exhilarating burn in his lungs. The cold made him feel alive and reminded him of the power of

God. The same God that made the wind blow had promised to be with him always. Even to the ends of the age. Even through the darkest times of his life. Nick needed to hold on to that, now more than ever.

By the time he stepped inside the diner, he could hardly feel his nose. The heat felt good, setting his cheeks to tingling.

"Hi, Josie." Nick greeted the waitress behind the counter. "Is my takeout order ready?"

"Sure thing, Pastor Nick. I'll go grab it for you." The young woman headed for the kitchen, but turned and came back. "Oh, hey, your wife's here if you want to join her. She's in that booth over there with her friend. Seems like they're celebrating something."

Almost against his will, Nick looked in the direction Josie had pointed. Maura and Rachel sat in a corner booth. They were eating cheesecake and laughing.

Laughing.

Blood pounded in Nick's ears. How could she be laughing? It was an irrational reaction, but he couldn't help it. She may have had years to deal with the death of their child, but for Nick the pain was brand new, his emotions raw like exposed nerves. To him, the child had died today. He couldn't imagine finding anything to laugh about.

Just nine months before, Nick had been living his life the best he knew how when she walked back into it. Nine months . . . enough time to have a baby.

Or to kill a dream.

Maura speared a piece of cheesecake. The fork was halfway to her mouth when she stopped and turned, looking right at him. Her face grew serious, and she set the fork on her plate with a clank. Across from her, Rachel stopped talking and craned her head around, her eyes wide as saucers when she saw him.

Rachel knew. Shame rose up, threatening to choke him. How many other people knew? How would he face his congregation once the inevitable gossip started?

From the booth, Maura raised her hand in a tentative wave. He turned away, taking his wallet out of his inside coat pocket. He paid Josie, grabbed the white paper bag, and stalked from the warm diner, back out into the cold, biting wind.

21

Jed Benson cleared his throat before announcing, "Miss Hattie left me the house."

Nick looked up from the portable communion kit he was repacking. "What was that?"

Jed muttered something under his breath. He was an odd fellow. A fifty-five-year-old man who owned his own house and land, he would make quite a catch if he ever ventured into Granger. But in all the years Nick had known him, he'd never gone past his own property line. Jed made people come to him, and even had his groceries delivered. Which is why Nick made it a point to visit and give him communion at least once a month. Or whenever Jed had new livestock that needed blessing.

Nick snapped the small leather case shut and put it in his briefcase. "What house are you talking about?"

"You know that old hovel about a mile from here? It borders my property. Miss Hattie owned the ten acres it sits on." He retrieved the battered Stetson he'd taken off earlier in respect of the communion ceremony and jammed it back on his head. "I tried to buy it from her more than once, but she was a stubborn old bird. Said she'd give it to me if I'd promise to start going to church."

Nick laughed. "That sounds like Miss Hattie."

Jed nodded. "The only reason I wanted to buy the land was so I could tear the old eyesore of a building down. But she was stubborn, and so was I. The last time we talked she said maybe she'd leave it to me in her will. I'll be darned if she didn't do just that."

Nick stood and Jed followed his lead. "Are you surprised?"

Jed shrugged. "After all those crazy hoops she made you jump through, I can't figure out why she didn't do the same to me."

"I guess she knew when to give up. She couldn't hound you anymore after she was dead." Nick walked to the door with Jed on his heels.

"Maybe. But I can't stop thinking about it."

Ah. That explained why Jed brought it up. "If you're feeling guilty, there's a simple way to remedy that."

"Didn't say anything about feeling guilty." Jed snorted. He didn't speak again until they reached Nick's car. "Thanks for stopping by, Pastor."

Nick stowed his briefcase in the backseat. "I'm glad to do it. But I'm still praying that one day, I'll have the privilege of sharing communion with you in the church."

Jed made no reply. He shook Nick's hand, gave a curt nod good-bye, and went back into his house.

Driving back to town, Nick thought about Jed. What in the world could keep a strong, capable man a virtual prisoner on his own property? Something traumatic must have happened to him, some emotional experience he couldn't shake. Nick fervently hoped that one day the man would feel he could share it with someone.

Nick thought of Maura. She'd been scarred by the miscarriage and had kept it to herself for years. How was it he felt compassion for Jed, but not for her?

Simple. Because the situation was totally different. Maura was his wife.

They hadn't spoken in three weeks. Buried in his work, Nick filled his days with meetings, lunches, and dinner appointments with members of the congregation and their families every evening. When he did have free time, he spent it in his office preparing for Easter services. The holiday came early that year, and he prayed the weather would hold for the annual sunrise service.

Still, there were those moments of silence when Nick couldn't escape Maura's presence, or the lack of it. When he came home at the end of a hectic day, the parsonage seemed quieter and emptier than it used to. Sometimes, he'd stand in the doorway of the guestroom, looking over the empty closet and the neatly made bed, and he'd ache at the loss of her. On Sundays, she was always in church, sitting in the back pew until after worship when she left with Lainie and the youth group. When he saw her, singing praises to God with the rest of the congregation, his heart yearned for her.

But then he remembered the secrets she'd kept, the lies between them, and the pain of betrayal shot through him all over again.

Nick arrived back at the church. He pushed thoughts of Maura aside as he gathered his belongings and went inside.

Pauline sat at her desk, but didn't offer him her usual smile. Instead, she gave a quick quirk of her lips as she thrust a stack of small pink notes at him. "Here are your messages. And I need your final version of the Easter bulletin. Please."

It was ironic that the two most blessed and enjoyed holidays on the calendar, Christmas and Easter, also created the most work in a church office. And the most frazzled nerves.

"Sorry to keep you waiting. I'll do that right away."

He shuffled through the messages as he went back to his office. Nothing there that couldn't wait until after he finished the bulletin.

Twenty minutes later the intercom on his phone buzzed. Pressing the button on his end, he answered, "I'm almost done, Pauline."

"That's great, but it's not why I'm calling. Lainie Waters is here to see you."

"Send her in." This was good. He had a question for her about the youth group skit anyway.

A moment later the door opened and Lainie bounded in. "Good morning, Pastor," she said, full of her usual energy and enthusiasm. "How are you doing?"

"Fine." He pointed at the chair on the other side of his desk. "Have a seat."

Lainie plopped down and began talking before Nick could say another word. "I'm concerned about a member of our congregation. And as pastor, I knew you'd want to know about it, right?"

"Of course. I—"

"Good." Lainie put her hands on the edge of the desk and leaned forward. "I've been watching this man for the last few weeks, going through the motions. He says he's fine, and maybe he even believes he is. But it's obvious to me that he's hurting about something."

Nick shifted in his chair. "Lainie, you don't have to dance around it. If you're talking about me, just say so."

Lainie sighed, her face a little sad. "Okay, it's you. I know something happened between you and Maura. I don't know what it is, and I don't want to know. But for the last few weeks, she's been depressed and you've been acting like . . . well, I've never seen you act this way before."

Nick clasped his hands together. "Lainie, I appreciate what you're trying to do. But what happened between Maura and me doesn't concern you or anybody else in this congregation."

"I disagree. People aren't stupid. They can see the tension between the two of you. If you don't mind me saying, you're not setting a very good example."

Had she just said what he thought she'd said? "Excuse me?"

Lainie didn't flinch. "By not dealing with the situation, you're acting like it's okay to ignore your problems."

That hurt. "I'm not ignoring anything. I may not be dealing with it the way you want me to, but I am dealing with it."

Lainie bowed her head. When she looked up, her eyes were devoid of their usual spark. "My mom and dad have been married for thirty-four years, but I don't think they've ever really loved each other. So when I see that two people who love each other as much as you and Maura do can't work it out and be together, it breaks my heart."

She stood up to leave. "By the way, I've asked Maura to officially be my assistant with the youth group. So you'll be seeing her around a lot more, maybe even at council meetings. Just thought you should know."

Nick's thoughts swirled as Lainie left his office. Was what she'd said true? Was he setting a bad example for the congregation?

As a pastor, he exhorted people to forgive each other. It was a foundation of his faith. He knew he had to forgive Maura, so he had. But if his forgiveness was genuine, why did he still harbor such anger and bitterness toward her?

Was forgiving someone because you had to the same as forgiving someone from your heart?

A Scripture from Ephesians exploded in his mind. *Be kind and compassionate to one another, forgiving each other, just as in Christ God forgave you.*

Nick bowed his head, conviction weighing down his heart. He'd told himself that he had dealt with the situation, but he hadn't really forgiven Maura. He'd pushed the pain and the hurt into a corner of his heart and covered it with something he called forgiveness. But that wasn't enough.

Nick stabbed the intercom button on the phone. "Pauline, the bulletin's fine as is. Go ahead and run it. Hold all my calls for a few hours, please. I don't want to be disturbed."

He grabbed his Bible. He didn't expect an instant fix, but he was finally ready for the Lord to change the attitude of his heart.

———✦———

"Excuse me. Pardon me." Maura made her way through the crowd of people standing in Randall Tucker's fallow cornfield. The sun was just cresting the horizon, illuminating the misty air.

The weather forecast for today had been favorable. A high of forty-five with light winds and only a ten percent chance of rain. You couldn't ask for much better in late March.

Maura smiled at the people around her. The Easter sunrise service was an annual tradition at Faith, and those who made a habit of attending were well prepared. They wore wool coats and scarves, earmuffs and knit caps, and waterproof footwear. The newcomers were easy to spot. They shivered in their fancy dresses and fine suits, and happily accepted the blankets and extra coats being passed out by the council members.

Maura was excited about her first Easter in Granger. Between the youth group and her classes at the theatre, she'd developed a strong drama team, and they were participating in the service. Only the situation with Nick dampened her enthusiasm. She'd hoped that if enough time passed, he would want to talk to her, give her another chance. But nothing had changed.

Her thoughts returned to the present as Oren Thacker stepped in front of her, his arms full of cold weather gear. "Christ is risen!" He greeted her.

"He's risen indeed!" Maura returned the traditional Easter greeting. She smiled at Oren and pointed to the blankets he held. "It's nice of you to have those handy. Are you ready for your monologue?"

"Absolutely. I'll meet you over there in a few minutes."

With a wave, Maura went to the barn where her drama group had gathered. It was warmer inside, although their breath still hung white and puffy in the air. She spoke to everyone, sharing hugs and encouragement. When Oren and Lainie came in, they stood in a circle and shared a prayer, finishing with a group cry of "Amen!"

Maura addressed them all. "Okay, when it's time to go out—"

The barn door opened and a blast of cold air knocked into her. She looked to see who came in, and her heart skittered in her chest. It was Nick.

The air in the room seemed to sizzle with electricity despite the cold. "Good morning, everyone. Christ is risen!"

"He's risen indeed!" Twenty voices answered the pastor in unison. Maura, whose throat had turned into a sandbox, silently mouthed the words.

"I hate to send you all out into the cold, but I need to talk to Maura for a minute." When it became obvious that no one was moving, he added, "Alone."

Maura watched her students practically run from the room. And did she catch a smile on Lainie's face?

The barn door shut with a dull thud.

Nick cleared his throat. "Maura, I've been thinking about us a lot this week."

She didn't trust herself to speak. She could only nod.

"Easter is a time of new beginnings," Nick continued. "I can't go out there and lead the congregation in this service until we work out our problems. I can't go on being married in name only. It feels deceitful. Like we're living a lie."

What did he mean? "I don't understand," she squeaked out.

He pointed to her left hand. "I need your ring back."

Maura swallowed the tears that threatened to fall. She wouldn't cry. She had no one to blame for this but herself. She peeled off her glove, slipped the engagement ring from her finger, and held it out to Nick.

His fingers folded around her hand as she placed the ring in his palm. "Maura, I forgive you, and I hope you can forgive me for everything I put you through. I made you feel like you were the least important person in my life. But that couldn't be farther from the truth."

Her heart pounded as he got down on one knee in front of her. "I love you, Maura, and I want to be your husband again. If you'll have me."

With a cry of happiness, Maura dropped to her knees and threw her arms around Nick. She slammed against him like steel against a magnet, almost knocking him to the straw-covered floor. Their lips met, hungry for each other and the reunion they'd been denied for far too long.

Reluctantly, they broke apart. Nick put his hand against her cheek. "I'm not a perfect man, but I promise to be the best husband I can, with God's help. I promise to love you and not take you for granted ever again."

She took his hand, drawing it to her lips. "I promise to talk to you and share with you, even if I have to grab you by the ear to do it. No more secrets between us. Ever."

Nick smiled. "Let's do this right." He reached into his pocket and pulled out the other half of the wedding set. "With these rings, I thee wed. Again."

A thrill coursed through Maura as Nick slid the rings on her finger. She reached out for his hand, removing the band that he'd never taken off. "I wed thee again too. Till death parts us." She slipped it back on his finger, where it belonged.

Nick stood, helped Maura up, and sealed their promise with a kiss. "We should get out there before people start wondering what we're doing."

He put his arm around her and they walked to the door. "Just one thing," Maura asked. "How did you get the other half of my wedding set?"

Nick grinned. "I still have a key to your apartment. I snuck in while you were at the theatre. And speaking of your apartment, what would you think about living there instead of the parsonage?"

Maura's head buzzed with excitement. Had she heard him right? "Really?"

"Sure. It's got an extra bedroom. We'll have plenty of room there, even when our family grows."

"Unless we have a bunch of kids."

Nick squeezed her close. "We'll cross that bridge when and if we come to it."

He pulled the barn door open, and they stepped outside. To Maura's amazement, the entire congregation stood in a semi-circle around the barn, facing them. Lainie and Oren stood in the front, the ring leaders of the group.

Nick kissed Maura on the cheek. He grabbed her hand and held it up high as if she was a winner in a prizefight, making her rings sparkle in the early morning sunlight. "She said yes!"

The congregation erupted in cheers. A few yards away, the choir started singing an impromptu a cappella version of Handel's "Hallelujah!" chorus.

Maura took in a deep breath, inhaling all the joy and exuberance surrounding her. On the horizon, the sun broke out in a riot of colors, igniting the sky like a fiery stained-glass window. Her heart swelled until she feared it would burst with happiness. With her husband beside her, and the congregation in front of her, Maura thanked God for the dawning of a new day, and for the second chance He'd given her and Nick.

Discussion Questions

1. Maura left Nick because she felt that she came last in his life. Do you think she had an unrealistic expectation of what it would be like to be a pastor's wife? Have you ever felt neglected in a relationship? How did you handle it?

2. As a new pastor, Nick felt obligated to spend most of his time on his job. Was he right to do this? How might he have better balanced his life? Was he right to expect Maura to immerse herself in church service as well?

3. There were issues in Nick and Maura's relationship that were never addressed. How might things have worked out differently for them if they had talked about their feelings? Do you find it difficult to talk through problems with your own spouse or those close to you?

4. Granger is a small, close-knit town. What are the pros and cons of living in that type of community? How did the town affect Nick and Maura's marriage?

5. Maura felt that Nick put his job before her. But when she takes over the theatre and finds a job she loves, she discovers how easy it is to be consumed by work. Do you think it helped her see Nick's side of the story? Have you ever been in a similar situation? Has your work ever taken over chunks of your personal life?

6. When Maura returns to town, she reconnects with her friend Rachel. Have you ever had a friend who looked past your faults and just loved you? Have you been that friend? Was it worth it?

7. At Christmastime, Nick gives Maura a teacup to replace the one he'd broken years earlier. What's the symbolism behind this gift?

8. When Maura discovers a lump in her breast, she immediately remembers her mother's battle with breast cancer. Have you ever gone through a comparable experience or helped a loved one through something similar? How did you feel?

9. Nick drops everything to be with Maura as she goes for tests and waits for results. Considering their history, why was that so important?

10. Maura kept her miscarriage a secret from Nick. What were her reasons? Was she right not to tell him?

11. When Nick finds out about the miscarriage, he feels betrayed and says that Maura lied to him. Is not telling someone the truth the same as lying? Did Nick overreact? How would you feel in a similar situation?

12. In the end, Nick and Maura realize they were both responsible for the problems in their marriage. Only through forgiving each other were they able to move forward. Have you ever experienced a seemingly irreparable rift with a friend or loved one?

Want to learn more about author
Jennifer AlLee and check out other great
fiction from Abingdon Press?

Sign up for our fiction newsletter at
www.AbingdonPress.com
to read interviews with your favorite authors, find tips
for starting a reading group, and stay posted on what
new titles are on the horizon. It's a place to connect
with other fiction readers or post a
comment about this book.

Be sure to visit Jennifer online!

www.jenniferallee.com

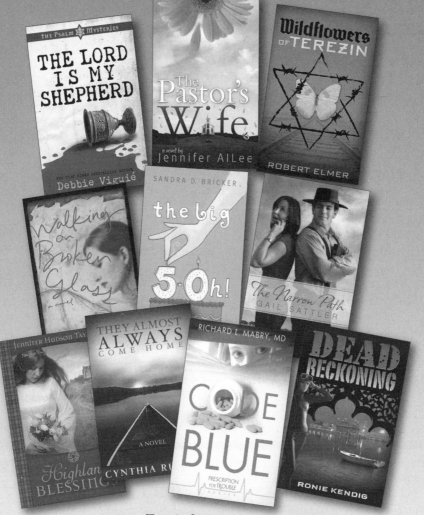

What they're saying about...

Gone to Green, by Judy Christie

"...Refreshingly realistic religious fiction, this novel is unafraid to address the injustices of sexism, racism, and corruption as well as the spiritual devastation that often accompanies the loss of loved ones. Yet these darker narrative tones beautifully highlight the novel's message of friendship, community, and God's reassuring and transformative love." —*Publishers Weekly* **starred review**

The Call of Zulina, by Kay Marshall Strom

"This compelling drama will challenge readers to remember slavery's brutal history, and its heroic characters will inspire them. Highly recommended."
—*Library Journal* **starred review**

Surrender the Wind, by Rita Gerlach

"I am purely a romance reader, and yet you hooked me in with a war scene, of all things! I would have never believed it. You set the mood beautifully and have a clean, strong, lyrical way with words. You have done your research well enough to transport me back to the war-torn period of colonial times."
—Julie Lessman, author of *The Daughters of Boston* series

One Imperfect Christmas, by Myra Johnson

"Debut novelist Myra Johnson ushers us into the Christmas season with a fresh and exciting story that will give you a chuckle and a special warmth."
—DiAnn Mills, author of *Awaken My Heart* and *Breach of Trust*

The Prayers of Agnes Sparrow, by Joyce Magnin

"Beware of *The Prayers of Agnes Sparrow*. Just when you have become fully enchanted by its marvelous quirky zaniness, you will suddenly be taken to your knees by its poignant truth-telling about what it means to be divinely human. I'm convinced that 'on our knees' is exactly where Joyce Magnin planned for us to land all along." —Nancy Rue, co-author of *Healing Waters* (**Sullivan Crisp** Series)
2009 Novel of the Year

The Fence My Father Built, by Linda S. Clare

"...Linda Clare reminds us with her writing that is wise, funny, and heartbreaking, that what matters most in life are the people we love and the One who gave them to us."—Gina Ochsner, Dark Horse Literary, winner of the Oregon Book Award and the Flannery O'Connor Award for Short Fiction

eye of the god, by Ariel Allison

"Filled with action on three continents, *eye of the god* is a riveting fast-paced thriller, but it is Abby—who, in spite of another letdown by a man, remains filled with hope—who makes Ariel Allison's tale a super read."—Harriet Klausner

www.AbingdonPress.com/fiction